Praise for the
DEADLOCK
Series

"Once again, P.D. Atkerson mingles edge-of-your-seat action with heart-melting characters that make me want to just wrap them up in a hug. (Even though they'd probably punch me if I tried it)"

-Angie Thompson, author of *Bridgers: A Parable*

"I fell for this book so fast. It was exciting, and I love how Gregory handles the problems in it. It was such a great book, full of heartwarming moments, and adventure. It's so well written, that you will keep turning the pages, always wanting more. So good!"

- Heidi Ho, member of KDWC

"Atkerson weaves a tale of hope, alternating fast-paced action with tender moments that mark the journey from the past to a promising future, doing it all with her trademark sarcasm. Gregory is one boy you won't soon forget."

- Mary P., author of Anything

Deadlock

by **P.D. ATKERSON**

Deadlock (Deadlock book 1)

Cover design and creation by P.D. Atkerson
With image by: Image by **Andy Choinski** from **Pixabay**
Edited by L.L.A.
Published in the United States of America

http://pdatkerson.blogspot.com

Dedication to:
To all those who have helped me get this far in my writing.

CONTENTS

CHAPTER 1

Spitting the blood out of his mouth, Gregory shoved himself back to his feet and turned toward his brother again. "That was a lucky shot," he growled, wiping his hand across his mouth as they began to circle each other again. "One I don't think you'll be repeating."

Grew shrugged. "It's payback for all the times you gave me a bloody lip," he said, smirking. "Hey! Maybe when we're done people will think you're me. I guess you're not all that after all." With that, Grew swung at Gregory again.

Dodging to the side, Gregory caught his brother by the arm. He brought his own arm up and pressed it against Grew's, then he twisted around and shoved him toward the ground.

They both hit the mat, and Gregory quickly rolled onto the top of his twin. But before Gregory pinned him down, Grew brought his leg up and wrapped it around Gregory's, then he twisted to the side and shoved Gregory off of him.

Gregory rolled back to his feet, a second later his twin brother followed suit, and they went at each other again.

Deadlock

Dodging and swinging at each other, blocking punches with their forearms and kicking out at each other, Gregory and Grew fought like mortal enemies.

Finally, Gregory swept his leg around, hooked it around Grew, and shoved him back. He was upon him the second he hit the mat, but before he could do anything more than pin him down, Gregory began to grow dizzy. "Whoa," he groaned, pressing his hand on his forehead as he leaned back and rested his head against the mat.

He wasn't sure what happened, but the next thing he knew Grew was free and standing over him. "What's wrong with him?" Grew asked, frowning as he glanced toward their instructor who was standing to the side of the mat.

Roman stepped forward and knelt beside Gregory. "Gregory, can you tell me what's going on with you?"

"I... I can't think straight," Gregory said, grimacing as he slowly sat up. "Roman, what's going on? You know, don't you?"

His friend and mentor moved over to his things and picked his water bottle up. Roman twisted off the lid and sniffed it. "Ah... That explains it," he mumbled, glancing over toward Gregory. "Congratulations, young Deadlock. It would appear it's time for your testing."

Gregory's stomach lurched, and his head seemed to spin even more than before. "Are you sure?" Grew said, speaking Gregory's exact thoughts. "But..." He frowned. "I'm the older brother, shouldn't I be the one who's tested first?"

Roman shook his head. "Don't be daft," he said. "You're only older by a few minutes, and you know your father has never cared which one of you was born first."

For as long as he could remember, Gregory had known this day was coming, but that didn't mean he was really ready for it. But as another wave of dizziness hit him, Gregory was forced to lie down again. "Roman, I… I'm not ready!"

"You're going to do fine," Roman whispered, kneeling next to him as he grabbed Gregory's arm and gave it a quick squeeze. "You've been training for this your whole life; I know you're going to pass."

"Right," Gregory said, sighing as he closed his eyes and allowed the darkness to engulf him.

By the time Gregory came back to his senses, he found himself cuffed to a chair in the middle of a small stone room, with mildew in the air and water dripping down the walls. The only light came from the lights embedded deep into the roof, behind a thick piece of glass.

Looking around, Gregory realized there was nothing else inside the room, and the only exit was through the metal door in front of him. Then, as if caused by him noticing the door, there was the grinding sound of metal on metal as the door swung out, and one man entered the room.

Deadlock

He had a short trimmed beard and dark eyes that bore into Gregory as he moved to stand in front of him, his hands clasped behind his back, a handgun sticking out from under his jacket.

Gregory's body stiffened as he gave the man a small nod and held his head up high. "Father."

"Hello, Gregory," his father said, crossing his arms over his chest as he frowned at him. "How are you feeling?"

"Like I've been drugged and cuffed to a chair," Gregory said, forcing himself to smile up at his father. "Thanks for asking."

He gave a sharp nod before reaching under his jacket and pulling out a file. He flipped it open and pulled a picture out.

"This man is known as the 'Preacher'," he said, holding the picture of a man in his early twenties out so Gregory could see it. "I want you to memorize his face because he will be your first target. He's caused us quite a bit of trouble, and for your test, you're going to make sure he doesn't cause any more trouble, by killing him. Fail, and I never want to see your face again."

Gregory swallowed and nodded. "Yes, Father," he said. "I won't fail."

His father nodded as he put the picture and file away and moved toward the door. "You have ten minutes," he said, glancing around as his hand wrapped around the handle. "Before this room fills completely with water. The door will be locked, and you'll need to find a way out before you drown. I'd say good luck, but you're a Deadlock; you *shouldn't* need it."

With that, Gregory's father shoved the door open and stepped out. The second the door closed behind him, water began to rapidly pour down the walls. *That explains the smell,* Gregory thought.

Moving quickly, Gregory slipped his arms free from the cuffs and jumped to his feet, his combat boots splashing in the water that was already starting to pool at his feet.

The door was obviously the only way out since there weren't any other doors or windows. But if it was locked, how was he going to get through it? He hurried over to the door and looked it over. It didn't take him long to realize they'd given him everything he'd needed.

The water was already soaking into his pants up to his knees as Gregory reached toward the bottom door hinge, bolted to the wall. He took the handcuffs that had held him to the chair and pressed them together around the bolt, working them like a wrench.

Gritting his teeth, he began to twist the handcuffs around. Slowly, the bolt began to move and twist out of the wall. By the time he was finishing the bottom hinge, the water had already passed it by a foot, and his jacket was soaked all the way up his sleeves.

Splashing through the water, Gregory moved back

toward the chair and grabbed it. Shoving the chair up against the door, Gregory scrambled up onto it and taking the handcuffs, he set to work again.

The water was freezing, and Gregory soon found himself shivering as he fought to keep a grip on the handcuffs. But after what felt like a lifetime, he finally pulled the last bolt out of the wall.

With shaking hands, he shoved the bolts and handcuffs into his pockets as the water level reached his shoulders, and he shoved off from the chair. He kept his face just above the water as it continued to rise, faster with every second.

It wouldn't be much longer before the room was completely filled, and he knew it. Still, he waited until the very last second before Gregory gulped in as much air as his lungs could hold and dropped beneath the surface just before it reached the roof.

Swimming deeper under the water, Gregory shoved the chair away from the door, then lay on his back and planted his foot against the door. Making sure to hold his breath, Gregory brought his legs back and slammed them back against the door. It vibrated, and Gregory saw a couple of bubbles, but it didn't break the suction.

By now, Gregory's lungs had started to burn as he brought his legs back again. He repeated this several times, each time taking much more effort than the time before. Then finally, with one more solid kick, the door broke free from the doorframe and fell away. And the next second, Gregory was swept forward by the water rushing out of the room.

He slammed against something solid and was knocked out before he saw what was on the other side of the door.

Chapter 2

Gregory's head was pounding when he finally opened his eyes again. Sitting up slowly, he ran his hand through his hair and found a small patch of sticky skin. When he pulled his hand away, the tips of his fingers were stained with blood.

"Great," he grumbled. His clothing was soaked, and he probably had a concussion, but at least he was still alive.

Shoving himself to his feet, Gregory glanced around him. After a second's hesitation, he turned left and headed toward the dim light at the end of the tunnel or wherever he was, his shoes squeaking as he walked across the wet ground.

It didn't take him long before he came upon the exit leading out into a forested clearing. Sitting next to the doorway was a duffle bag. Kneeling beside it, Gregory unzipped the duffle bag and found a change of clothing inside.

He quickly changed into them, topping it off with the

baseball cap and gun at the bottom of the bag. Once he was finished, he shoved his wet clothes back into the back and kicked it into the corner.

After that, he didn't wait around inside the cave (which he'd come to realize was a mine shaft) any longer. He'd heard enough stories to know that his testing had already begun and sticking around there wouldn't be a very good idea on his part, especially if the shaft turned out not to be all that safe after the water had gone flooding through it.

Stepping forward, Gregory exited out into the forest clearing and looked around him. Now to decide what direction he should head. It was late afternoon, and the sun was shining down from the horizon in front of him, which meant north was to his right and south to his left.

With a nod to himself, Gregory turned to the right. North was the best direction to head in, especially if he ended up having to travel at night. That way he could continue to follow Polaris after dark, assuming he could see it through the trees.

Shaking away these thoughts, Gregory quietly started forward. It didn't take him long, though, to realize someone was following him. He kept walking and pretended not to notice. They were good, which probably meant they were sent by Deadlock. But even with their DL training, he could still tell they were there.

He'd gone through several minutes of them following

him, when without missing a beat, he twisted around, caught onto a tree branch. and began to climb up the tree. Within a matter of seconds, he was above eye level.

Gregory was balancing carefully on a branch high up in the tree when the two men appeared below him. He didn't know their names, but he recognized them as members of DL. But not anyone who had been close to his family. *What are they doing here?* he wondered. He'd never heard of anyone interfering with a testing.

"Where'd he go?" the man on the left said, spinning around in a circle. "I thought he went this way."

"If I knew where he was," the other man growled, "we'd already have him, and we'd be on our way back home."

Gregory hesitated a second before bending forward and leaping off the branch. He landed with a soft 'thud' behind the two men, who quickly turned toward him, grabbing for the guns at their sides.

"What are you two doing here?" Gregory asked, pulling out his own gun at the same time as they aimed theirs at him. But he kept his grip steady as he continued to point his toward the nearest man.

"Impressive, really," the man said, grinning as he took a step closer to Gregory. "I didn't expect you to get out of there quite so quickly. I had thought you'd be a little bit more waterlogged first, though. Too bad it doesn't matter now."

"Put your gun away," the other man ordered as he did just that, and the first man followed suit a second later. "There's no reason to be so uncivilized, is there? I'm Thomas and this is Adam, and well, we both know who you are. Don't we, Adam?"

"If you know who I am, then you should know not to get involved in my testing," Gregory growled, keeping his gun on them even though they'd put theirs away. "The Deadlock blood flows through my veins, and you would be wise to remember that."

"Blood's not everything," Adam said, gritting his teeth as he stepped toward Gregory. "You're just a boy, yet your father wants to make you a leader of Deadlock, and we're not going to let that happen. We're not going to take orders from a *child.*"

Gregory's instincts instantly kicked in, and he jumped back a step. "Stay back!" Gregory ordered, aiming the gun at Adam. "I won't hesitate to shoot you. If this is part of the test…"

"Stupid boy, this isn't part of your *test,*" Thomas snarled. "Not that it would matter. You won't be finishing your testing." The next second, they both leapt at him and grabbed hold of his arms before he even had a chance to fight back.

Gregory struggled against them, but he couldn't break free from their grip as they threw him onto his stomach and pinned him down. One held his arms against the ground

Deadlock

while the other did something Gregory couldn't see.

"You're going to pay for this!" Gregory hissed as he continued to fight them.

Adam laughed as he pressed something against his neck. "No, but we will get *paid,*" he said, just as something small poked Gregory's neck and a moment later, the world around him began to grow foggy.

"That's it, relax…" Thomas purred, chuckling to himself. "As much as we would enjoy it, we won't be killing you by a bullet in the head. We've got to make it look like you failed your test."

"Good thing there's a creek near here," Adam said, laughing as he loosened his grip on Gregory. Not that it did Gregory much good. His mind was in a fog as they roughly duct-taped his hands together and gagged him.

They yanked him to his feet and half carried, half dragged him through the forest and away from where they'd stopped. It wasn't much longer before they came upon the creek they'd mentioned earlier.

But in Gregory's opinion, it wasn't a creek. It was a fast-moving waterfall! Tied up and gagged, it would be almost impossible for Gregory to survive the current. Gregory tried to break free, but he couldn't fight strongly enough against them, and the gag in his mouth muffled his yells.

He dragged his feet, but it didn't seem to do him any good as they pulled him forward. "See you at the bottom,"

Thomas whispered into Gregory's ear before he gave him a hard shove in the center of the back and pushed him over the edge.

Gregory fell through the air for only a second before he hit the water and his vision was quickly filled with murky water, but the freezing temperature was exactly the shock he needed to wake himself up and kick whatever drug they'd given him out of his system.

More water! Gregory thought, fighting the current as it threatened to drown him. *Is this some kind of sick joke or something?* He shook away those thoughts as he was swept past a cluster of rocks and was just barely able to catch hold of it.

Twisting around, he braced himself against the largest rock on the top, then proceeded to use the rough edges on top to cut through the duct tape binding his wrists together as he continued to fight against the water pulling at his slowly numbing limbs.

Back and forth he rubbed them between his legs as his lungs began to burn and black spots appeared in his vision. Finally, the tape snapped, and Gregory lost his perch on the rock.

With one final rush, the water seemed to slow down, and Gregory was able to grab hold of the edge of the creek and pull himself up the side. Coughing, Gregory yanked the gag out of his mouth and gasped for breath as he fell

Deadlock

forward and onto the damp, pine needle covered ground.

Was he really still alive? Gregory actually found that hard to believe as his heavy breathing came in and out, fog rising from his mouth. Shivering, he slowly shoved himself into a sitting position and looked around.

He'd lost all sense of direction, thanks to the two DL traitors, and the sun had since been covered up by thick clouds. He was trying to decide which way to go when he heard the sound of running footsteps behind him.

With one glance over his shoulder, Gregory's eyes locked with Thomas' who stood on the other side of the rushing creek. He spun around and started to run, stumbling as the blood began to pump through his numb legs again.

"You can't escape, Gregory Deadlock!" Thomas yelled after him. "We're going to kill you, even if it doesn't look like an accident! You will die! There's nowhere you can hide from us." But Gregory barely heard him as he ran.

Chapter 3

Reaching the top of a rise in the mountainside, Gregory leapt off the small edge at the top of it and fell the ten feet to the forest floor below. He rolled to his feet and started to run again, pine needles and small branches clinging to his clothing as the wet fabric itself stuck to his skin.

He wasn't sure how long he'd been running before he stumbled upon the road and heard a sound in the distance. It took Gregory a second to realize the sound was a car speeding toward him.

"Great," he mumbled before spinning around and throwing himself out of the way of the car. He hit the ground hard, knocking the air out of his lungs and whacking his vision out for a second.

"Oh my gosh!" he heard a muffled voice cry. The sound of a slamming car door, but at the moment Gregory didn't really care as his eyes rolled into the back of his head and stopped fighting the exhaustion.

He felt someone wrap an arm around him and lift him

off the ground, but by then the drugs the DL members had put into his system took full effect, helped by the drop of adrenaline, the cold, and exhaustion finally hitting him all at once, draining him of any fight he might still have had in him.

"It's alright, you're safe," the voice said as Gregory felt himself placed down against something softer than the ground he'd been on a moment before. A door slammed again and a second later, Gregory heard the sound of an engine starting up before he felt a hot breeze blow against his face.

It took Gregory a second to come back to his senses, and he realized he was sitting in the passenger seat of a car.

Gregory looked over at the man in the driver's seat and instantly pulled away from him, hitting his head against the window as he cursed the stupid drugs in his system. The man was the Preacher! The man Gregory was there to kill.

"Whoa! Calm down," the man said, holding onto Gregory's shoulder as he pushed him back against the seat. "It's alright, I'm not going to hurt you. Just calm down before you hurt yourself."

Gregory did calm himself, but not for the reasons the man wanted him to. He needed to think, and freaking out wouldn't help with that.

The man gave him a small smile as he pulled his hand away. "What's your name, kid?" he said. "If you don't mind me asking."

Kid? Gregory thought, frowning. *Right*. He'd forgotten people outside of Deadlock considered people his age as kids. But 'kids' weren't trained to kill like he was. And even though this man was his target, he was also the only way he could get out of there and away from Thomas and Adam.

"Gregory," he finally said, figuring if in the near future he killed the guy, he might as well know his real name.

"Nice to meet you, Gregory," the man said, smiling as he held out his hand to him. "I'm Jonathan Winfield."

Gregory stared down at the man's hand and fought back a laugh. *Ironic*. The gesture to see if someone was armed, and the man didn't even know he was doing it. "Hello," he said, ignoring the hand as he glanced out the window and realized Adam and Thomas might not be that far behind him.

"What are you doing out here, Gregory?" Jonathan asked, glancing out the window. "Is there someone out here with you?"

"What?!" Gregory said, his gaze snapping to Jonathan. "Why would you say that?"

"I just meant, you shouldn't be out here alone," he said. "Who knows what kind of whackos are out here!"

"You mean, like you?" Gregory asked before he could stop himself. He bit his tongue and knew his father would have punished him for not keeping his tongue in check.

Jonathan laughed. "Fair point," he said. "If your parents are near here, I'm sure we can find them…"

Deadlock

"No, they're not here!" Gregory snapped when he spotted a shadow moving in the forest where he'd come from. "Can we just go, please?" he asked, scooting down in his seat. "There's no one with me." *That I want to see again.*

He studied Gregory for a second longer before nodding, putting the car into gear, and starting down the street. "Alright, we'll go," he said. "Then we'll figure out a way to contact your parents."

"You won't be able to," Gregory said, closing his eyes. "My mother's dead, and unless you know something I don't, you won't be able to find my father." With that, he pretended to fall asleep. He knew there would be questions later, but for the moment he'd do his best to avoid them.

Somehow, Gregory must have dozed off at some point, because the next thing he knew, the car was slowing down and pulling up in front of a house. "This is my house," Jonathan said, shutting the car off and pocketing the keys.

Gregory just nodded as he looked out the window. It looked like a normal enough house. Not that he knew much about those kinds of things. After his and Grew's mom died, they'd spent all their time at the Deadlock training base deep in the Rocky Mountains.

Clearing his throat, Jonathan opened his car door. "Come on," he said, climbing out of the car. "You can meet my wife. This is going to be fun to explain," he mumbled under his breath, obviously not expecting Gregory to hear him.

Not sure what else to do just yet, since the man was his target, he decided to do as the man asked and go into the house. Gregory made sure to keep his jacket over his gun as he climbed out of the car

Shivering, he followed the man to the door. During the ride in the car, Gregory had forgotten how wet he was, and the cold night air wasn't helping matters. As he tugged his jacket down, Gregory momentarily thought about drawing his gun and finishing his testing right then and there. Yet, he couldn't do it. He couldn't put his finger on it, but there was something about the man that he'd never seen in anyone before.

The fact that he'd stopped to help him unnerved Gregory, but oddly enough, not in a bad way. Gregory wanted to wait and find out what the man wanted from him, then he'd finish what he was sent there for. What would a couple of hours matter anyway? He caught a lucky break anyway; he doubted that his father would have expected the man to pick him up.

You never know what serial killer you might pick up, Gregory thought, snorting to himself. *Or a trained assassin.* Shaking away that thought, Gregory hunched his shoulders against the cold as he waited for the man to open the door and motion him inside.

"Sorry about the boxes," Jonathan said, shoving a pile of them out of the doorway as he stepped through. "We just moved here, and it's kind of a mess." Gregory just nodded

Deadlock

as he looked around and mapped the place in his mind.

After about half a second, Gregory decided that other than the door itself, the window across the room would probably make the best escape. But even that would be hard to use, considering the amount of stuff he'd have to climb over to make it to the window.

"Esther!" Jonathan called, pulling off his jacket and tossing it onto a hook next to the door. "I'm home, and… um… I brought a guest."

"What?" a woman said, wiping her hands on the apron she wore as she stepped into the room. She stopped when she saw Gregory. "Honey? Who's this?" she asked, glancing toward Jonathan with a tight-lipped smile.

Jonathan returned the smile. "Esther, can we talk in the kitchen?" he asked. "Gregory, make yourself comfortable while we talk. I think we might have candy in a bowl in here somewhere; you're welcome to look around for it."

"Sure," Gregory said, running his hand through his still-damp hair as he pretended to look around for the candy. As soon as the two of them moved toward the kitchen and disappeared through the swinging door, Gregory made his way toward it.

Gregory stood next to the door, just close enough that he could hear through it, but not so close that he'd get hit by the door if they were to come back out through it. He closed his eyes and strained to listen.

"I know what you're going to say…" Jonathan started.

"Oh? And what is that?" Esther asked, cutting him off. "That you went to town for eggs, not another kid?!"

There was a pause, and Jonathan cleared his throat. "Okay, maybe not exactly what you were going to say," he said. "But what did you expect me to do? He was freezing and wandering alone in the woods when I found him. Did you want me to just leave him out there?"

"And do you know why he was out there?" Esther asked.

"No," Jonathan admitted, and Gregory made note that he needed to keep an eye on the man's wife. "He wasn't exactly talkative on the way back here either. He's just a kid; I didn't think I needed to give him the third degree."

Esther let out a long sigh. "Doesn't he have somewhere he could go?" she asked. "I'd rather not have his parents think we kidnapped him!"

"I don't think so," Jonathan said. "And by the sounds of something he said… I don't think his parents are going to be a problem. Well, not a problem in the way you think." Before he could hear any more, Gregory felt someone watching him, and the hairs on the back of his neck stood up.

"You shouldn't be eavesdropping," a boy said behind him.

"And what are you doing?" Gregory asked, before turning around to face the boy. "Just being a casual

Deadlock

bystander?"

The boy blinked and tilted his head, his thick dark curls bouncing. "A what?" he said, frowning. Gregory was just about to answer when Jonathan and Esther reentered the room, and he was grateful he'd stayed away from the door when the edge of it swept past his arm, missing it by an inch.

CHAPTER 4

If they noticed that Gregory was eavesdropping, they didn't show it as they turned toward him.

"So, Gregory," Jonathan said, clasping his hands out in front of him. "How would you feel about staying for dinner? Then we can discuss your um… parents later? I for one am starving! Well, not starving…"

It wasn't until that moment that Gregory realized how hungry he was. He glanced toward the man he was sent there to kill, and he bit his lip. It wouldn't hurt to wait a little longer, right?

"What do you have to eat?" Gregory asked, crossing his arms as he turned toward the man's wife.

Esther laughed. "You're a teenage boy; I doubt it matters," she said, then motioned him forward. "Come on, the dining room is this way." Gregory stiffened when she took his arm and pulled him gently down the hallway. "Jackson, why don't you go get Mia and tell her we're eating." Before Gregory could even say anything, Esther led

Deadlock

him into another room, this one clean of all the boxes. "I hope I made enough," she said, giving her husband a pointed look. "But I suppose we'll make it work."

Just then, a little girl came running into the room and screamed. "Daddy, Jackson pulled my hair! Make him stop."

Instinctively, Gregory had twisted around and grabbed for the gun nestled against his spine but didn't draw it, and he was glad when he heard why she'd screamed. *Seriously?* She'd screamed because the boy had pulled her hair?

Gregory sighed and relaxed his arm back at his side. Thank goodness he'd never had a sister.

"Mia, this is Gregory," Jonathan said, sweeping the little girl up in his arms. "He's our guest, and I want you to behave while he's here. Alright? No more screaming," he added in a whisper, before kissing her on the cheek and sitting her back down.

The little girl bobbed her head up and down, causing her bangs to bounce. "Yes, Daddy."

Daddy? Okay, Gregory had wondered about Jackson being their son, but he was a hundred percent sure 'Mia' wasn't their daughter. She looked *nothing* like Jonathan or Esther. Her Asian heritage was obvious, and though Jackson's slightly darker skin wasn't quite as much, he didn't look much like them.

"Are you here to live with us?" the little girl asked, looking up at Gregory with her big brown eyes.

"Alright, honey," Esther said, cutting in before Gregory

could even think of a response to that. "Why don't you take your seat?" she said, pushing Mia gently toward the table as she turned and headed into the kitchen again.

Hesitating, Gregory glanced around as he moved toward the table. He followed suit when everyone else pulled their chairs away from the table and sat down. He couldn't even remember the last time he'd eaten a meal around a table. It was long before his mother had even gotten sick.

"Mia, do you want to pray for us?" Jonathan asked once Esther had returned with several dishes of food.

Gregory glanced around and frowned. *Pray*? These people still did that? It would seem so, especially when they started to close their eyes. There was no way he was going to make himself that vulnerable around these people.

Fingering the steak knife, Gregory glanced toward Mr. Winfield, who just sat there, his eyes closed, unaware of how easily Gregory could finish him off. With just one swift movement, he could finish his testing in less than a day and be done with all of this.

It was at that moment that something happened to Gregory. His head started to pound loudly in his ears, and a cold shiver ran up and down his spine. Maybe staying in his wet clothing hadn't been a good idea after all.

Fighting back a groan, Gregory barely heard Mia starting her prayer and almost missed the end.

"And thank you for bringing us a new brother," Mia said. "Amen."

Deadlock

"Mia," Jonathan said, a warning tone to his voice as he gave the little girl's hand a squeeze.

"What?" Mia said.

"He's just a guest, remember?" Jackson said, rolling his eyes. "At least that's what Mom and Dad are claiming now, though I think they said the same thing about you."

Jonathan sighed. "He is just a guest." But that didn't seem to satisfy them, and they went on like that.

Esther was the only one who noticed that Gregory was acting weird. "Are you alright, sweetheart?" she asked, frowning as she tilted her head to get a better look at him.

"What? Oh, yeah, I'm fine," Gregory mumbled, squeezing his head between his hands as he tried to stop the pounding. There was no way he was going to tell her that his head felt like it was going to explode.

Pressing her lips together, Esther glanced toward Jonathan. "Are you sure?"

Knowing she wouldn't leave him alone, he gave her the best answer he could think of, the truth. "Yes, I'm just... tired and..." Gregory sneezed and grimaced. "Still a little cold from falling in the creek."

"What?!" Esther cried, her eyes growing large as she twisted around toward Jonathan and swatted him on the back of his head. "You didn't tell me he fell in a creek! What else did you forget to tell me?"

Jonathan ducked out of her reach before she could swat him again. "I didn't know!" he said. "I just thought he was cold when I found him."

"You mean he's still wearing his wet clothing?!" she cried, shoving her seat back and jumping to her feet. "What were you thinking?"

"Well, it's not exactly like I had a change of clothing for him," Jonathan said, climbing to his feet a moment later.

"Go get something for him to change into," Esther said, shaking her head at her husband as she moved around to where Gregory was sitting. "It will probably have to be something of yours; I doubt he'd fit any of Jackson's clothing."

"Yes, ma'am," Jonathan said, grinning as he saluted her and hurried out of the room. He returned a minute later with a pile of clothing in his arms. "Here," he said, holding them out to Gregory. "These should work for you."

Gregory hesitated a second before taking the bundle from the man and standing up. The fact that they seemed to care that he was wet was just weird for him, and Gregory wasn't quite sure what to do.

"Why don't you go change, and then we can finish eating?" Esther said, giving Gregory a soft smile. "The bathroom's the first door on the left. You can go in there and change."

"Right..." He hesitated a second, before deciding changing into dry clothes wouldn't be a bad idea. He tightened his arms around the bundle as he turned and headed down the hall in the direction Esther had indicated.

Deadlock

Once inside the bathroom, Gregory closed and locked the door. He took in a deep breath and leaned against the counter. What was wrong with him? He could have killed Jonathan and already be out of there by now.

Shaking away those thoughts, Gregory pulled out his gun and placed it on the counter, then quickly changed into the too-big clothing from Jonathan, a sweater and pants. After making sure sure his gun wasn't visible when he slid it under the sweater, Gregory unlocked the door and went back into the dining room.

When he stepped back through the French doors, the man and his family were sitting around the table again, obviously waiting for him. Not sure what else to do, Gregory sat back down and fought the urge to bounce his leg.

His head wasn't bothering him quite as much as it had been, but he still didn't feel so good. And once they started to eat, he began to feel much better. But his chance to get rid of Jonathan easily had already passed.

"It's getting late," Esther said, once they were all done eating. "I think it's the little ones' bedtimes." Both Jackson and Mia groaned, and Gregory used that as a distraction as he slipped the knife off the table and into his sleeve, making sure the blade didn't cut through yarn.

"You can stay in my room!" Jackson said, beaming as he bounced up and down. "You can even have the top bunk. Right, Dad?"

"Jackson, we haven't even talked to Gregory yet. Is that

alright with you, Gregory?" Jonathan asked, turning toward him. "You can stay here with us, or if you have somewhere else to stay…"

"No, I don't have anywhere else," Gregory said, shaking his head. It was the truth; he didn't have anywhere to go until his testing was done. Besides, staying the night would give him a chance to finish his testing without anyone else around.

"In that case, I think Jackson will gladly share his room with you," Esther said, smiling as she stood up. "Why don't you show him where it is and get yourself ready for bed? I think we've all had quite the exciting night."

Gregory covered up a snort with a cough. She had no idea.

CHAPTER 5

It was a little unnerving, watching as Mrs. Winfield tucked Jackson in and offered to do the same for Gregory. He almost punched her for just suggesting it. But he didn't, because he figured that might make them a little less willing to let him stay the night.

Instead, Gregory shook his head and said no, quickly grabbing onto the ladder and scrambling to the top. He lay sprawled out on top of the sheets and stared up at the roof, grateful when Esther finally left.

Once the door closed behind her, Gregory rolled over, finding that lying on a gun wasn't the most comfortable way to rest. How long should he wait? He really had no idea if these people were deep sleepers or not. But the last thing he needed was for one of them to catch him sneaking around their house.

So he waited.

When he heard the odd noise coming from the bed under him, Gregory bent over the edge and looked down. It was obvious Jackson was asleep, so that was a start. At least he wouldn't get caught leaving the room.

Quietly, he slipped over the edge of the bunk and dropped himself down silently to the ground, skipping the ladder altogether. With one last glance to make sure Jackson's mouth was still hanging open, Gregory crept toward the door.

Inching the door open so it wouldn't make any noise, Gregory slipped out through it and quickly closed it behind him. With a glance down both sides of the hallway, Gregory made his way toward the room he'd spotted earlier and guessed was Mr. and Mrs. Winfield's.

The door was left open, so that would be helpful for him. In fact, this might be too easy. He was going to have to come up with a crazy story to tell his father when he got back. As he lay down on his stomach, the floorboards groaned.

"Did you hear that?" Jonathan's voice carried from the bedroom as Gregory began to crawl forward.

Esther sighed. "Maybe one of the kids got up to get a glass of water?"

"We just put them to bed."

Gregory blocked out their voices as he crawled through the doorway and into the bedroom. He sat up and moved to stand next to the wall, waiting to see if they'd notice him standing there. He had a feeling they wouldn't.

When they didn't say any more, Gregory took the

opportunity to edge his way toward the large dresser deeper into the room and drop down beside it. Since they were both still awake, he'd just have to wait.

Luckily, the little corner next to the dresser wasn't all that uncomfortable.

Scooting closer to the dresser, Gregory rested his head against it and closed his eyes. In the back of his mind, he could hear the ticking of the clock in the hallway, telling him how fast time was passing.

It was nearing midnight when Gregory decided they were asleep enough to try to take Jonathan out. He shoved himself to his feet and stretched out his aching limbs as he rolled his shoulders.

Once he could move his arms without the sensation of pins and needles, Gregory reached behind him and pulled the gun out from under his sweater.

Ignoring the slight tremble in his hands and the spike in his heart rate, Gregory took a step toward where Mr. and Mrs. Winfield lay sleeping. He reached the bed and slowly made his way around to Jonathan's side, fingering the gun the whole time.

Gregory took in a deep breath and flicked off the safety, but caught himself. He'd need a quick escape if he didn't want to kill Esther too. Glancing around, Gregory moved toward the nearest window and quietly opened it, then he turned back toward Jonathan and raised the gun.

He told himself it was the cold that caused him to shiver

when he lifted the gun and pointed it toward the sleeping man.

Groaning, Jonathan rolled over so he was now facing Gregory with his eyes still closed. And from the rise and fall of the man's chest, Gregory knew he was still sleeping, but something about seeing the man's face stopped him from being able to pull the trigger.

The man's eyelids flickered open and closed a couple of times, and Gregory knew he was waking up.

Retreating quickly, Gregory hid in the shadows, his heart thudding against his chest as he pressed himself up against the wall. If he was caught, there was no way he could explain what he was doing, especially with the gun he held in his hands.

Jonathan yawned and opened his eyes. He shivered, looked toward the open window, and frowned. "It's almost winter," he grumbled, shoving himself out of bed and toward the open window. "You really shouldn't be opening the window right now."

Esther sighed and rolled over toward him. "I didn't open it."

Closing and locking the window, Jonathan hurried back to bed. "Well, someone had to have," he said, shivering. "And I doubt one of the kids just snuck in here and did it."

Gregory waited until the man had made himself comfortable, then he turned and bolted silently out of the room and down the hallway to the bathroom. He shut and

Deadlock

closed the door, then leaned heavily against the counter again.

He looked at his face in the mirror and fought the urge to punch it. What was wrong with him? He should have just shot the man and gotten it over with. If he had, he could have been on his way home now.

But now he couldn't.

He knew he'd messed up big time, and if his father were there, he would be so ashamed of him!

Suddenly finding it hard to breathe, Gregory dropped to his knees and gripped the gun with both his trembling hands. *Okay...* He needed to think. Just because he'd messed this opportunely up didn't mean there wouldn't be another one. He'd just need to keep his head and make sure the Winfields didn't figure out why he was really there.

That should be fairly easy; they didn't seem to be the type of people to be suspicious of others. Too bad for them.

Looking down at the gun in his hands, Gregory realized he couldn't exactly sleep with it. He needed to find a place to hide it until he could decide what he should do next. Glancing around, Gregory spotted a vent in the wall above him.

The bathroom probably would be the best place for him to hide it, since it would be the easiest place for him to slip off to.

Placing the gun down on the counter, Gregory grabbed onto the edge and pulled himself up onto it, careful not to fall into the sink as he reached up toward the vent. He was glad to find the screws loose as he began to untighten them.

Once he had it off, he placed his gun inside and put the cover back on, careful to make sure the screws were exactly the same place as they'd been. With that done, he jumped back down off the counter and straightened his clothing out.

Now all he had to do was pretend to be a normal kid until another opportunity came up.

Exiting the bathroom, Gregory hurried back toward Jackson's room and slipped inside. He fought a sneeze as he entered the bedroom, but couldn't fight it back for long, and he was just reaching for the ladder to the top bunk when he sneezed.

Jackson rolled over and opened his eyes. "What's going on?" he mumbled, rubbing his eyes as he looked up at Gregory.

"Nothing," Gregory whispered, glancing toward the door. "I was just coming back from the bathroom. So go back to sleep. That's what I'm going to do."

Jackson slowly nodded as his eyelids slid closed again. "Oh… okay."

Gregory waited until he was sure the boy was asleep again, before grabbing the ladder and scrambling to the top. This time he slipped under the covers and tried to make himself comfortable, but that wasn't an easy task normally.

Deadlock

Rolling over, Gregory stared at the roof, wondering what Grew was doing. Not that it mattered. He was sure Grew didn't care what was happening to him. For all his brother knew, he could be dead, drowned in the first part of his testing.

He wasn't even sure what had brought his brother to his mind, since he barely ever thought of him. It wasn't as if they were close. They didn't hate each other, but there was no love lost between them.

But it wasn't either of their faults. If anyone was to blame, it was their father. He'd always been the one to put a wedge between them, having them compete against each other with everything they ever did.

Ever since their mother died, there hadn't been a reason not to. Trying to make their father proud seemed to be the only thing they both had in common anymore. It was with those thoughts on his mind that Gregory slipped into a dreamless sleep.

CHAPTER 6

Gregory was yanked from a light sleep with someone hovering over him. His eyes flew open, and he leapt toward the person.

"Whoa!" Jackson cried, his eyes growing wide, and Gregory realized he was holding the boy's wrist tightly in his own hand.

"Don't do that!" Gregory warned, reluctantly releasing the boy. "What were you doing anyway?"

"I...I was just going to tell you that we eat breakfast early on Saturdays," the boy stammered. "What was that?"

Ignoring the boy's question, Gregory glanced toward his watch. It was already five past seven. How had he slept that late?! He couldn't even remember the last time he'd done that, even after a rough training session with Roman. "Well," he said, turning toward the boy. "Just don't do it again, alright? I'm a very light sleeper, and... I sometimes react before I can even think about it. Clear?"

The boy nodded. "Okay."

Deadlock

"Good," Gregory said, shoving his sheets back. "Now, please. Get out of my face." A couple of minutes later, Gregory was out of bed and heading into the dining room. He stopped and headed into the living room when he saw someone sitting on one of the couches.

As it turned out, it was the little girl he'd met the night before. Mia? Yeah, he was pretty sure that was her name. Looking over at her, he realized she was playing on a Gameboy, but part of it looked like it was torn apart.

Frowning, he glanced toward the girl again. "What are you doing?" he finally asked, stepping toward her.

"Well, this Gameboy's programming is messed up," she mumbled, clicking away on the device. "I'm just fixing it."

Gregory crossed his arms and looked over her shoulder. "You can do that? I mean, can anyone actually reprogram a… Gameboy you called it, like that?"

"Yes, and yes, I can," she said, still working away at it.

"Aren't you like… six?" Gregory asked, squinting at her.

"Five and eight months," she said, looking up and grinning at him. "But thanks. It's always fun when people think I'm older than I am."

"Right," Gregory said, nodding as he glanced around to make sure no one else was around. "Are you like some kind of genius or something?"

Mia laughed. "Mommy and Daddy say so, but they think everyone's special."

"Right," Gregory said nodding. He didn't know a ton

about programming himself, but she might be useful in Deadlock. He'd have to keep that in mind when he finished his testing. "Well…" Before he could say anything else to her, Mrs. Winfield entered the room, and he snapped his mouth shut.

"There you two are!" Esther said, smiling at them. "Breakfast is ready, and Mia, I made pancakes."

The little girl's face lit up as she tossed the Gameboy down and scrambled to her feet. "Pancakes!" she cried, running from the room, barely missing plowing into Mrs. Winfield as she did.

"Do you like pancakes, Gregory?" Esther asked, laughing as she turned toward him.

Gregory shrugged. "Um… honestly? I don't know what they are. So… I guess I have no idea."

Esther stared at him. "Your mom and dad never made them for you?" she asked, obviously surprised by that, and Gregory didn't have a clue why. But the thought of his dad cooking anything was hilarious to Gregory, and it took a lot of effort on his part not to laugh.

"Yeah, no," Gregory said, shaking his head as he grinned. "My parents weren't exactly the cooking type." From what he'd heard over the years, the food they ate was illegally bought from the US military. He quickly decided that probably wasn't something he should tell her though.

"Well, I guess you're in for a treat then," Esther said, smiling as she hooked her arm through Gregory's and pulled him out of the living room. In the dining room, Jonathan, Jackson, and Mia were all sitting around the table, eating and talking.

Jonathan looked up at them when they entered. "Sorry, honey," he said, laughing and shaking his head. "We already prayed and started to eat, because apparently, Mia couldn't wait five minutes to eat her pancakes."

"I didn't know how long they might be!" Mia said, her mouth full of pancakes as she went to shove another forkful in.

"Now, sweetheart, do slow down before you choke," Esther said, letting go of Gregory's arm and hurrying toward the little girl. Unsure of what else to do, Gregory took the empty seat he'd used the night before and sat down.

As it turned out, the pancakes resembled something he'd had before, but they tasted nothing alike. Then again, the meal the night before had been like nothing he'd had before. These people's food actually tasted pretty good.

Soon, he was done eating and glanced around the dining room. He watched the family and realized they actually seemed to enjoy talking to each other while they ate. And the odd thing was, they seemed to just talk about what was going on with their lives.

For as long as he could remember, his father had only asked him about his training, and most of that he learned from Roman anyway. Mr. Winfield even asked Mia how it was coming with the Gameboy she was reprogramming.

Even though it was obvious he really had no clue what she was talking about, he still seemed to care.

None of it made any sense to him! He tugged at the collar of the sweater he was wearing and grimaced. Maybe it was just him, but it was sure getting warm in there.

"So, Gregory…" Esther said, glancing toward Jonathan as she cleared her throat. "Do you have someone you want us to call to come and pick you up? Your mom or dad, maybe? Or maybe an aunt or uncle?"

Gregory shook his head. "No, I don't have any aunts or uncles," he said. "And we don't have a phone. Not one I would know the number to, anyway."

"Really? Did you grow up in a cult or something?" Jackson asked, wiping syrup off his face.

"Jackson!" Esther said, shooting the boy a look. "Don't be rude! Mind your manners."

"What did I say?" Jackson asked, looking around the table.

"What's a cult?" Gregory asked, frowning. He was as confused as the boy was about why Esther was upset about what he'd said.

"Well… I've actually never had to explain what a cult was before," Jonathan said, frowning as he rubbed his chin. "I guess you could say it's a group of people who are overly devoted to a person, idea, or even a movement. That kind of thing," he said. "They usually live together in a secluded area, working, eating, and doing everything together."

Gregory thought about it for a second, and it sounded like Deadlock was a cult to him. "That sounds about right," he said, shrugging. "I guess I grew up in a cult, Jackson."

Jonathan choked on his food and glanced toward his wife, before turning toward Gregory. "Gregory, cults are… bad things," he said. "Dangerous things, and… if your family's a part of one…"

"We really need to talk about it more before we can let you go back in good conscience," Esther said, grabbing Jonathan's hand and giving it a squeeze.

Gregory sat up stiffly as he wrapped his hand a little tighter around the fork he was holding. "I wasn't aware that I asked if I could leave," he said, gritting his teeth as he forced himself to keep his voice level.

"We're not saying anything against your family, Gregory," Esther quickly said. "It's just… we would be worried about you, that's all."

"Is Gregory from a cult?" Mia asked, glancing around the table. "Is he crazy?"

"No, honey," Esther said, glancing toward Jonathan.

So what? They thought they were better than him because of how he'd grown up? He was starting to see why his father wanted to get rid of the man! "I guess it doesn't matter then, that you can't contact my father by phone," Gregory said, shoving his seat back. "If you'll excuse me, I'm going to get some air." Without waiting for them to respond, he marched out of the dining room and didn't look back.

But he wasn't actually going outside, not yet anyway. Instead, he stopped outside the door and pressed himself up against the wall, listening for the conversation he knew was going to be coming.

"What do we do?" Esther asked.

"I think I'm going to call, um… our friend," Jonathan said. "See what he thinks about all of this. Maybe find out more from Gregory."

Esther sighed. "That sounds like a good idea," she said. "If he is from a cult, I really don't want to send him back there."

"Yeah… I wanted to talk to you about that."

CHAPTER 7

It was so ingrained in Gregory to stay in shape that later that day he found himself heading out of the house and toward somewhere where he could train. Fall had already come, so there was a bite to the wind as he headed out, and Gregory ignored it as he pulled off his jacket.

Then, without pause, he swept his leg around and kicked out at the tree. The next second, his foot connected with the tree, and he pivoted around and shoved himself off the tree. He flipped upside down and landed on his feet again.

He twisted around and punched at the tree, repeatedly for several minutes. By the time he was finished, Gregory grimaced and wiped the blood off his knuckles onto his pants. Maybe he was taking a bit more anger out than he'd originally meant to.

Gregory wasn't even sure what he was trying to work out, but something was bothering him. Shaking away that thought, Gregory moved toward the tree again. He grabbed onto the thick branch hanging above his head, then he curled his legs up and began to lift himself up to chest height and back down again.

His arms were just beginning to shake when Gregory heard footsteps and quickly dropped himself back to the ground and twisted around to face the intruder. Who turned out to be Jonathan Winfield.

What does he want now? Gregory wondered, gritting his teeth. With one swift movement, he could kill him and this would be all over. He could go home, a hero. Finishing his testing in record time. But something stopped him. He thought of the knife tucked in his sleeve, but he did not draw it.

"Is there something you needed?" Gregory growled out as he turned back to the tree and thought about punching it again.

"No, I just thought I would come out here and see what you were doing," Jonathan said, shoving his hands into his pockets.

Gregory nodded. "Well, now you've seen it," he said. "So, what are you still doing out here?"

"What are you doing? I mean, *why* are you doing this?" Jonathan said, motioning to the tree.

Gregory shrugged. "My father is… was… insistent about always being in shape," he said. "And this is how I stay in shape."

Deadlock

Jonathan whistled under his breath and shook his head at him. "I can barely get Jackson out of bed before noon," he said, then he laughed and nodded toward the house. "Unless we're having pancakes of course."

"If I didn't get out of bed when I was told to, my father would have taken away my bed." For some reason, Gregory felt like he shouldn't have said it the second he did. Jonathan's body had gone stiff, and he frowned at him. "Did I say something wrong?" Gregory asked. "Or does this have something to do with the 'cult' you were talking about?

"No, well, yes. It's just…" Jonathan sighed and rubbed his face.

"Am I supposed to guess what it is? Or something?" Gregory asked, taking his jacket and wiping his face off with it. "Because I've always been bad at guessing games."

"Right, sorry," Jonathan said. "I was just wondering… How old are you?"

Gregory hesitated.

Not only was that not something he'd been expecting, but he was trained not to give away any personal intel. But after what the man and his family had done for him, he felt like they at least deserved to know a little bit about him. "I'll turn thirteen in a few months."

"*Turn?*" Jonathan said, staring at him as he shook his head. "You're… you're not even thirteen yet?"

Gregory shook his head. "No, sir."

Jonathan rubbed his face again and shook his head. "You seemed older to me," he said. "I just assumed…" He sighed and shook his head.

He really wasn't sure if he was supposed to respond to that or not, so Gregory decided against it and just studied the man.

"Have fun… doing whatever it is you were doing," Jonathan said, stepping back. "Just don't stay out here too long; it's starting to get cold, and you might still be fighting something off after you fell into… was it a creek?"

Fun? Gregory wasn't sure that's what he would call it. He forced a smile. "Sure," he said. "I'll make sure not to stay out here too long." *Though I'm not sure why you'd care.* With that thought, Gregory turned back toward the tree at the same time as Jonathan turned and headed back to the house.

Instead of hitting the tree this time, though, Gregory went through the different fighting moves Roman had taught him and Grew over the years, silently working his way through an imaginary fight.

Soon, Gregory knew that if he kept at it much longer, he would drop. That's when he decided maybe it was time to go back inside and take a break.

Huffing, he rolled out his shoulder and turned toward the house, where an expensive car stood in the driveway.

He didn't know much about his new housemates, so

Deadlock

he'd assumed it was their car. Now he wasn't sure.

The hairs on the back of his neck stood up, and he glanced around, grateful not to see the car's owner in sight, but that also meant they were most likely inside the house. For a second, Gregory wished he hadn't put the gun in the bathroom vent.

But it was too late to have those kinds of thoughts, so instead, he silently made his way back through the trees toward the house. When the time came for him to finish his testing, it would come in handy that the Winfields lived deep in the woods. Far from any other houses, and any witnesses.

Turning the front door handle slowly, Gregory slipped through the door and glanced around. A suit jacket hung next to the door, and he was sure it hadn't been there before. Gregory moved deeper into the house, and he could tell something was different, even before he saw the man sitting in the living room talking to Jonathan and Esther.

Gregory wasn't sure if it was even possible, but the hairs on the back of his neck seemed to stand up even more when the talking stopped the second they saw him entering the room.

It didn't help things when they all turned toward him, and he instantly knew they were talking about him. "Did I miss something?" he asked, crossing his arms and narrowing his eyes toward the man. He wore a crisp white suit and navy tie, too well put together for Gregory's liking.

"No, you didn't miss anything," Jonathan said, climbing to his feet as he glanced toward the man. "We were um… just talking."

"Yes," Esther said, jumping to her feet too as she grabbed Jonathan's hand. "Honey, why don't you help me make lunch?"

"Good idea," Jonathan said, giving her hand a quick squeeze as he turned toward Gregory again. "Why don't you two chat while we get the food ready? I'm sure you can find *something* to talk about."

"Good idea," the man said, nodding as he studied Gregory. "I'd like to get to know you, Gregory. Sounds like you've had an adventuresome twenty four hours. I'd love to hear other stories you might have to tell."

Without waiting for Gregory to respond, both Jonathan and Esther scurried out of the room.

So subtle, Gregory thought, rolling his eyes as he stepped into the living room and flopped down onto the couch. He really should have just killed the man and gotten it over with. It would have saved him a lot of trouble.

"So… you work for the government," Gregory said, crossing his arms as he glared the man down and leaned back against the couch.

The man looked surprised Gregory had figured that out so quickly, or maybe at all. But in reality, it hadn't been all that hard for him to figure out. The car the man was driving was a dead giveaway.

Slowly, the man nodded. "Yeah," he said, studying Gregory. "I'm Special Agent Benjamin White. Jonathan and Esther are friends of mine."

So this was the friend he'd heard them talking about after breakfast, and they obviously thought he was a danger after all.

"So... FBI," Gregory finally said.

CHAPTER 8

Agent White laughed and shook his head at Gregory. "Yes," he said. "I do work for the FBI. How did you know that?"

"That's easy. Because you're the only ones who call yourselves 'special' agents," Gregory said, snorting as he continued to study the man closely. "So, what does an FBI agent want from me?"

Tilting his head, the agent gave Gregory a fake smile. "What do you mean?" he asked. "What would we want from you?"

"Do we have to play this stupid game?" Gregory asked, huffing as he ran his hand through his hair and turned his gaze away from the agent, and opted instead for studying the design in the wood roof.

The agent sat up a little straighter. "Are we playing a game, Gregory?" he asked. "Because I don't even know the rules."

Having the agent act like he didn't know what was going

on was getting old very quickly. "Esther and Jonathan didn't just leave the room for no reason," Gregory said, shoving himself to his feet as he stepped toward the agent. "They wanted us to be alone for some reason; that was obvious."

"Maybe," Agent White said, shrugging as he slowly followed Gregory's lead and climbed to his feet.

"There's no maybe about it," Gregory said, clenching his fists at his sides. "So? What do you want from me?"

The FBI agent hesitated a second, and Gregory wondered if he was really going to try and continue to deny. But the agent didn't. "Fine," he said. "Esther and Jonathan asked me to talk to you, that's all."

"Right," Gregory said, flashing the agent a smile. "And have we talked enough to satisfy them?"

Agent White laughed. "Have we talked?" he asked.

Gregory shrugged. "As much as we're going to, no matter *what* you might try." He'd passed his anti-interrogation tests with flying colors, and a lot of blood and bruises. Since the man was an FBI agent, he doubted there was anything he could do to him that he hadn't already been through.

"I just want to know if you're in any trouble, Gregory," he said, taking a cautious step toward him. "From what the Winfields told me you said today, it sounds like you might be in a bit of trouble if you don't go back. Is that true?"

"I'm not going to spill my guts about my family," Gregory said, gritting his teeth as he took a step closer to the agent. They would have been standing face-to-face if Gregory wasn't much shorter than the agent, not that he noticed. "You can do what you want with me, but if you make an enemy of me, you will regret it."

The agent looked down at Gregory and raised an eyebrow. "I'm just here to help you, Gregory."

Gregory laughed and poked the agent in the chest. "And how exactly are you going to do that? You know what? Never mind. For a second there I thought I cared," he said. "But then it turned out to be a yawn. And guess what? I'm not afraid of you."

Agent White laughed. "I can tell." Finally, the agent was the first one to take a step back from him. "Well!" he said, still studying Gregory. "I'm going to go say goodbye to Jonathan and Esther."

Gregory remained silent as he stood where he had been and just waited.

Still shaking his head, the agent turned and headed down the hall toward the kitchen. No doubt to give Jonathan and Esther an update on what he'd learned about Gregory.

He waited until the agent was out of sight before he spun on his heel and lunged toward the nearest window. He yanked it open and quickly pulled himself through it, landing silently on the wet grassy ground outside.

Careful to make sure his shoes didn't squeak, Gregory crept around the side of the house and to the back where the kitchen was. Luckily for him, it looked like Esther had left the kitchen window open. Staying low, he crept toward it and pressed his back up against the wall beneath it.

"So? What did he say, Ben?" he heard Esther's voice.

"Nothing," Agent White said with a soft laugh. "He knew I was a federal agent the second he saw me. I wish some of my men were that tightlipped. In fact... I think he found out more about me than I did him."

"Was he really that hard to talk to?" Jonathan asked.

Agent White laughed again. "I've had computers that were more receptive to conversation, Jonny," he said. "Yes, he was hard to talk to."

Esther sighed. "Well, thank you for at least trying."

"Yes, thank you," Jonathan said. "But I assume you didn't learn anything about where he comes from, or if it's safe for him to go back there?"

"Yeah..." Agent White cleared his throat. "I don't think he should go back to wherever he's from. There's just something... off about the kid. He's definitely not scared by anything, that's for sure."

"Is that a bad thing?" Esther asked.

"No," the FBI agent said. "Not by itself, but I just wonder what's made him that way. It takes some odd events to make a kid like that, and I'm not sure I want to know what those events are."

"So, you really do think he's from a cult?" Jonathan asked, his voice barely above a whisper.

"A cult," Agent White agreed. "Or… maybe something worse."

Gregory had heard quite enough. "I think it's time I left," he mumbled to himself as he shoved away from the wall and hurried back toward the front door. Careful to avoid running into the FBI agent, he slipped back into the house and into the bathroom.

Climbing onto the top of the counter, just like he had the night before, Gregory opened the vent and reached inside. The gun felt colder than Gregory remembered it being as he wrapped his hand around it and pulled it out of the vent.

Swinging his legs around, he sat on the edge of the counter and checked the cartridge as he glanced toward the door. What was he doing? He was letting himself get comfortable here, and he really shouldn't.

He needed to finish his testing, he knew that, yet something still stopped him, and Gregory knew exactly what it was.

The Winfields were so normal, and it was nice.

Strange, but nice.

He'd never had normal, but he also knew it was something he'd never have. And why should he? He was a Deadlock! Far superior to anyone else. His father, with the help of Roman, had pounded that lesson into him more times than he cared to remember.

Holding the gun out in front of him, Gregory closed

Deadlock

his one eye and lined up the sight. All it would take was six pounds of pressure to pull the trigger, then it would be game over for Mr. Jonathan Winfield.

Too bad pulling the trigger was the easy part.

No, the hard part was making sure no one caught him, and dealing with the aftermath of all of it.

"Just do it!" Gregory growled to himself, lowering the gun as he shoved himself off the counter and turned to look at himself in the mirror. Unfortunately, the boy looking back at him didn't feel much like a killer. But he had to be.

He needed to bite the bullet (figuratively of course) and get this over with. The longer he waited, the harder it would be. He could not, no he *would* not get attached to them. It was bad enough that he knew the man's name and those of his family.

It made the job harder when you made the target more human than they should be. His father would be disappointed in him for letting it get this far, but not as much as he would be if he kept it going.

If he really wanted to become a part of Deadlock, he needed to finish his testing, and he needed to do it now, not in a day or even an hour.

It's now or never.

Pulling his shoulders back, Gregory tucked the gun under the sweater he was still wearing. Then he reached for the door and stepped out of the bathroom. He would find Jonathan, and no matter what, he would finish this. For his father, and for everything he knew.

CHAPTER 9

Gregory's pulse was surprisingly steady as he stepped out into the hallway and looked both ways. He was starting to wonder where to head when he heard the commotion coming from the living room.

Tugging at his sweater to make sure the gun was covered, Gregory stepped down the hallway and out the front door. He crept around the side and toward the window looking into the living room.

If Jonathan was in there, it would be the easiest way to get rid of him, since a bullet could easily break through the glass and kill the man. Moving up to the wall and stepping around the windowsill leading to the window in the basement, Gregory peeked around the curtain and into the living room.

There Jonathan was, in the center of the room. Unfortunately, he wasn't alone. Mia stood there giggling as she clung to Jonathan's neck, while Jonathan himself was wrestling with Jackson.

Deadlock

Gregory didn't understand why, but it was obvious they were just playing. But what was the point of wrestling if it wasn't to pin your opponent down and beat them up a bit? It wasn't a good wrestling match unless *someone* was bleeding, at least that was what his father always said.

He moved to pull his gun out from under his sweater, and with steady hands, he lifted it up and aimed it through the glass toward the man. But as he wrapped his finger around the trigger, he hesitated. Something he'd never done in practice.

But this wasn't practice anymore. Could he really take away Mia and Jackson's father? *Not take away, kill.* When he knew what it was like to lose a parent?

The thought of his mother's last days flashed through his mind. He hadn't even been there when she died because his father had sent him away for a couple of days of training, saying it wouldn't matter if he was gone such a short time.

It had mattered.

Grew had still been there, and he said she had passed away peacefully in her sleep.

Yet, Gregory's chest still hurt any time he thought of her, and the fact that he never got to say goodbye and that he'd never see her again. Could he really do that to the two little kids, who'd obviously lost, or never had, families before the Winfields?

Gregory tried to reason that he wasn't really their father,

but he couldn't. Not while watching them in there, playing. Something he and Grew had never done with their own father.

It barely registered in Gregory's mind when the three of them left the living room, at least not until the front door opened and he was yanked back to reality.

Scrambling, he turned his back to the window and tucked his gun behind him, covering it again with the sweater, hoping they wouldn't notice he was perched above the hole leading into the basement window.

On second thought, he shoved himself away from it as Jonathan and the kids exited the house. Glancing around, Gregory realized that anything he did to look casual was sure to backfire and make him look anything but.

Instead, he opted for just standing there. He was glad when the three of them quickly spotted him.

"Hey, Gregory. I was wondering where you went off to. Do you want to join us?" Jonathan asked as he helped Mia pull on her jacket and glanced toward where Gregory was standing. "We're going to go for a short walk through the woods, probably visit an old cabin the kids found that they like to play in."

"What?" Gregory said, squinting at the man. *What an odd waste of time.* "Oh, um… no thanks." With that, he headed back into the house, giving Jonathan one last glance as he did so. He needed to finish his testing, and maybe this little 'walk' was exactly what he needed to do it.

Deadlock

It didn't take Gregory long to find his jacket that Mrs. Winfield had hung up to dry the night before. Quickly, he changed out of the sweater that wouldn't blend in quite as well in the forest as the jacket he would now be wearing.

As soon as he had his jacket on, he headed back out the front door and scanned around him. Jonathan and the kids were already halfway down the driveway, but that wasn't the way Gregory was going to go anyway.

He cut to the left of the house, wormed his way through the trees, and crossed the street. Most likely the Winfields would be using the road to get to wherever they were going, at least for a little bit, and even if they were paying attention, they wouldn't be expecting Gregory to be coming from the other side of the road.

With his hood up, Gregory slipped from tree to tree, watching as they made their way down the road, soon breaking off onto a dirt trail most likely made by animals. Yet, they continued moving at a pace that was almost painful for him to match, even through the thickening trees as he found himself dodging branches every step.

Luckily for Gregory's sanity, they soon came upon the cabin Jonathan had mentioned earlier. It was surrounded by trees, and Gregory was't exactly sure it looked very safe. The kids went into the cabin, but Jonathan stayed outside, which worked out well for what Gregory had planned.

Once he was sure they weren't going to go anywhere any time soon, Gregory moved toward one of the trees far enough away from the cabin that Jonathan wouldn't easily see him, but close enough that he could see him.

Grabbing one of the lower branches, Gregory swung himself up and silently climbed roughly ten feet, halfway up the tree.

Neither Jonathan's posture or his face registered that he'd heard a thing as he continued wandering around the outside of the cabin. Gregory didn't really blame him for not wanting to go inside; the cabin didn't look like it was very tall, at least not anymore.

Perching on one of the thicker branches, Gregory pulled the gun out from under his jacket and pressed himself up against the tree trunk, fingering the gun as he glanced toward Jonathan again.

Gregory took in a steadying breath and allowed his eyes to close for a second.

He'd get to go home soon. *Home…* Was that really what Deadlock was to him now that his mother was gone? It was his life and everything he'd ever known, but it wasn't really home. Not anymore.

But right now, none of that mattered. He needed to do this, and he needed to do it now. If he did, he could take the shot before the kids came back out. At least that way they wouldn't have to see him die.

Opening his eyes, Gregory shifted his grip on the gun, placing the palm of his other hand under it as he took the safety off and aimed the gun toward where Jonathan was standing and had finally stopped pacing.

Taking in a small breath, he tightened his finger and pulled the trigger, but at the last second, his hand gripping the gun shifted to the side. The bullet went wide and slammed into the corner of the cabin, sending pieces of aged wood flying in every direction.

What did I just do? Gregory wondered, lowering his gun as his mind started calculating what he should do next.

"Mia, Jackson!" Jonathan yelled, running toward the door of the cabin, obviously aware of how close he'd been to being shot. "We need to go home, now. I never should have brought you out here during hunting season."

Hunting…? "Oh," Gregory whispered to himself. The man thought the bullet was from a hunter? That meant Gregory needed to make his escape while Jonathan was still inside the cabin; that way he'd still have another chance to finish his testing at a later time.

Without hesitation, Gregory shoved himself away from the tree trunk, leapt from the tree, and rolled across the ground and back to his feet, barely regaining his balance before he took off in a straight line in the direction of the Winfields' house.

Hurrying into the house, Gregory glanced around and tried to decide what he should do next. It was then he realized he was still holding the gun in his hand. It probably wouldn't be a good idea to still be holding that when the Winfields got back.

Quickly tucking the gun under his jacket again, Gregory untied his boots and kicked them off. He placed them on the mat next to the door, both perfectly straight with the laces tucked inside. Clean and orderly, like his mother always told him to be, one of the few things both his parents agreed on.

He was just finishing when he heard footsteps just on the other side of the door as someone ran up the steps of the deck leading up to the house.

Bolting down the hallway, Gregory ducked into the living room, just as he heard Jonathan open the front door as he called to his wife. "Esther!" he said. "I need your help here, Honey!"

It was then Gregory heard the sound of soft crying coming from the other side of the wall. *Who's crying?* he wondered, frowning. He knew for a fact that he hadn't hit anyone. He heard quick footsteps, then Esther gasping. "What happened? Why's Mia crying?"

"There must have been a hunter out there that thought we were deer," Jonathan said. "One of them almost hit me while I was waiting outside the cabin. Mia's just a little scared, but she wasn't hurt."

"Are you and Jackson alright?" Esther asked as Gregory heard her move toward Jonathan and take Mia from him. Gregory still didn't understand why the little girl was crying, especially if she hadn't been hit.

If Gregory or his brother had ever cried for anything

Deadlock

other than a *deep* flesh wound, their father would have made sure they got something worth crying over. He was yanked from those thoughts when he heard Jonathan say they should go into the living room and talk about it.

CHAPTER 10

Before the Winfields could enter the living room, Gregory leapt toward the nearest couch and tried to make himself comfortable, stretched out across it. Yet when Esther did enter the room, he could tell she was too distracted by Mia to even notice that he was already in the room.

"Did something happen?" Gregory asked, sitting up.

"Gregory!" Esther said, placing her hand over her heart as her other arm tightened around Mia, who was clinging to her side. "When did you come in here?" she asked, slowly letting her arm drop as she glanced toward Jonathan.

"I was here the whole time," Gregory said, the lie easy enough for him to tell them as he pulled his feet under him and slouched to his right against the back of the couch. "Did something happen? Why's Mia crying?" he asked, even though he already knew the answer.

He was the reason she was crying.

"Oh, nothing," Jonathan said. "Let's just say, our little

walk turned out to be much more eventful than I was expecting." Gregory just nodded, deciding that saying anything would probably be a bad idea.

As soon as they sat down on the other couch and seemed to be distracted talking to each other, Gregory got up and quickly left the room, bolting down the hall to Jackson's bedroom. He closed the door, and for a second, he rested back against it, taking in a slow, steadying breath.

Shoving himself away from the door, he moved toward the bunk bed. Grabbing the edge, he pulled himself up and swung himself over onto the bed. Pulling out his gun, he checked to make sure the safety was on, then tucked it under his bed and laid down. What was wrong with him?! Finishing his testing shouldn't be this hard.

Stupid, stupid, stupid! he chanted as he gripped his head and fought the urge to turn and hit it against the wall, repeatedly.

What was wrong with him?!

He'd had the perfect chance to take the man out, yet he hadn't. He'd messed up the shot like an amateur!

Sitting up again, Gregory wrapped his arms around his legs and pulled them up against his chest, resting his chin against his knees. It was times like these that he really missed his mother. She always knew what to say to make him feel better.

Yet, there was also a small part of him that still remembered how his mother used to hate the part of his training that was meant for him to learn how to kill someday. When he was really young, she'd tried to stop it, but after bringing it up with his father, she ended up with a bruised cheek for her efforts, and she never brought it up in front of him again.

That didn't stop her completely, though; there were several times she made him and Grew miss their training, every time coming up with an excuse when Gregory knew the truth. If she was so against him learning how to kill, what would she think about what he was doing now?

"Mommy, why couldn't you still be here?" he whispered. Though to who? His mother was gone, dead, and he'd never see her again. She was only just a hole in his heart now, nothing more.

Killing had never been something Gregory wanted to do, any more than his mother wanted him to. Deep down, he knew that he hadn't really missed shooting Jonathan outside the cabin. He'd moved his hand because he really didn't want to kill the man. But if he didn't, he could never go home.

But was Deadlock really a home to go back to? Had it ever been? The Winfields barely knew him, yet they'd been nicer to him than anyone, other than his mother, his whole life.

It was in that moment resolve formed inside of him.

He wouldn't do it. He wouldn't kill the man who had shown only kindness to him. When had his father ever

Deadlock

shown any emotion other than anger and disappointment?

Gregory was still thinking about his father when there came a knock from the bedroom door. Rubbing his eyes, Gregory quickly straightened out his legs and sat up. "Come in," he said, clearing his throat. He wasn't sure what else to say; after all, this wasn't his room, and privacy wasn't allowed in Deadlock.

A second later, the door opened and Mr. and Mrs. Winfield entered. Esther glanced toward Jonathan before moving toward the bed and giving Gregory a small smile. "We didn't get a chance to talk to you after Ben left," she said.

"Oh, so you want to 'talk' to me too?" Gregory asked, crossing his arms as he scooted his back up against the wall. "If you wanted to know something, you should have just said something to me, instead of sending that man to interrogate me."

"Oh, honey!" Esther said, reaching out to Gregory, but stopping herself. "That wasn't what he was doing. He was… well, he was just trying to get you to open up. I suppose some people might consider that interrogating, but that's not the way we wanted you to feel!"

"I'm sorry, that was me," Jonathan said, sighing as he moved closer to the bunk bed and leaned against it. "I thought… you might feel more comfortable talking to him than you would us. People seem to like talking to him."

Gregory snorted and slowly uncrossed his arms as he

played with one of the blankets. "I would be more comfortable hugging a cactus than talking to a government mouthpiece, like *Special* Agent White," he mumbled. "Agents aren't really the kind of people I would want to talk to about my personal life."

Esther patted his hand with hers. "We just want to know what kind of ghosts you're dealing with," she whispered. "So we can help you."

Ducking his head, Gregory tried to decide what he should do or say next. "My history is… complicated," he finally said. "And most of it, I'd rather not talk about."

"We're starting to see that," Jonathan said, biting his lip. "And we're not going to force you to tell us anything."

Gregory was about to say something when he ended up sneezing instead.

"Oh dear," Esther said, placing the back of her hand against his forehead. "You feel warm. Why don't you lie down for a bit?"

Gregory brushed her hand away. "I'm fine," he said, frowning at her. Why did she care anyway? She barely knew him; why did it matter to her if he was a little 'warm'? All the exercise he had that day probably had something to do with it.

"There's actually a reason we wanted you to talk to Ben," Esther said, glancing toward Jonathan again.

"We don't care who you were before we met," Jonathan said, placing his hand on Gregory's shoulder and giving

Deadlock

him a quick squeeze. "If your home isn't somewhere you can safely go back to, well, we would like you to stay with us... um... until you can find somewhere else to go, of course."

"Seriously?" Gregory said, squinting at them. "Why? Why would you do that? Like you've already admitted, you don't even know me." *You don't know why I'm really here*, he thought, grimacing.

"What Jonathan is trying to say is... we would *like* you to become a part of our family," Esther said. "But only if that's what you want," she quickly added, holding up her hands as her eyes grew big.

It took Gregory a moment to digest what she'd just said. "You... what?" he said, squinting at them.

Jonathan gripped the edge of the bunk bed and locked eyes with Gregory. "We've been praying about it."

"Since last night, in fact," Esther said with a small laugh. "And we've both feel like this is what God wants us to do. Even if it may seem a bit out of the blue, and we already have Mia and Jackson..."

"If you truly don't have a home to go back to." Jonathan glanced toward his wife. "We want you to stay here with us, to be a part of our family. Even take our last name, if you want to." He laughed. "We don't even know what yours is."

"There's been something missing in our family, and we think it's you, Gregory," Esther whispered. "What do you say?"

It made him feel a little stupid, but Gregory just couldn't wrap his mind around what they were saying. "You… *want* me to be a part of your family?" he said. "Why?"

Jonathan frowned, then slowly smiled. "You seem surprised."

"Of course I'm surprised!" Gregory scoffed, shoving himself away from the wall and closer to them. "My own father didn't want me. If I didn't perform better than Grew… Well, he would have had an easy replacement."

Both of them grimaced, and Esther reached out and squeezed Gregory's hand. "We can't say we know why your father… why he would treat you that way, but we promise you, you are wanted here."

Gregory studied their faces. Thanks to his years of training, he knew they weren't lying, and his chest tightened. Maybe… maybe there was still a chance he could have a normal family.

Finally, he swallowed and slowly nodded. "If you really want me to stay," he whispered. "Then I'll stay."

CHAPTER 11

The next couple of days went by in a blur for Gregory as he found himself slowly fitting in with the Winfields. Even though there were still a lot of things he didn't understand about them, like the strange picture of a bearded man they had hanging in the living room.

Was he an ancestor of theirs or something? he wondered, but never asked. Yet, it was still a little creepy having the picture staring at them as Gregory dealt out the cards for another game of 'War' against Mia, which he won in just a couple of minutes.

"It's a game of chance!" Mia cried, pounding her fist against the ground. "You shouldn't be able to always win! We've played four games, and you've won every time! How?"

Stifling a laugh, he glanced toward Jackson and gave him a wink. "I guess I'm just lucky?" Gregory said, shrugging as he shuffled the cards again and turned back toward Mia. "Do you want to try again?"

She huffed and nodded. "Yes, because at some point

you have to lose."

"We'll see, won't we?" Gregory said, his fingers slipping inside the deck as he flipped the cards around without ever looking down at what he was doing. At least that's what Mia thought. She had no idea when he fanned the cards out before 'shuffling' them, he just happened to memorize them first.

So maybe it wasn't the nicest thing to do to an almost six-year-old, but Mia made it too much fun to stop. And it wasn't exactly like he was hurting her by doing it, now was it? It was just a harmless game.

At least that's what he thought until they reached the end of the next game. "Daddy, Gregory's cheating!" Mia yelled, throwing her cards down as she jumped to her feet.

Jonathan looked up from behind his newspaper and sighed. "Mia, how could Gregory cheat at War?" he asked.

Gregory schooled his face as he felt an odd twitch inside, and he ducked his head. His father would have been proud of him for fooling someone, but for some reason, Gregory had mixed emotions now. Should he be glad he was able to fool her or not? Nothing was making sense anymore.

"Well... I don't know how he's doing it," Mia pouted. "But he is. I know he is!"

Luckily for Gregory, before anyone could say any more, the front door opened, and Esther hurried inside. She stepped into the living room carrying several bags.

Deadlock

Jonathan raised an eyebrow. "I didn't think you were going shopping."

"I stopped by the Klines' on the way back home," she said, placing the bags onto the living room floor and shaking her head at him. "It's actually stuff for Gregory." Esther turned toward Gregory and smiled. "Mrs. Kline had some of her son's clothing that he didn't need anymore. They should fit you. Do you want to see?"

"Um.. sure," Gregory said, shuffling the cards into a neat pile and standing up.

Esther quickly handed one of the bags to him and smiled. "Do you like them?" she asked as Gregory looked inside. The clothes consisted of a couple of T-shirts, jackets, and pants.

They looked to be his size and were neutral colors, which was good. The last thing he would have worn was something of bright colors. Gregory shrugged and looked up at Esther. "Well, they're functional."

Esther's shoulders slumped. "Oh."

Even without his training to read body language as easily as he could read a book, he would have known his words hadn't been the ones she'd been hoping for. "I didn't mean that in a bad way," he said. "That's the only kind of clothes I've had. I... I don't really know what to judge them by otherwise."

Giving him a small smile, Esther nodded. "I understand."

"I'm sure they're… da bomb," Gregory said. Wasn't that what Mr. Leer said the younger generation said that meant 'cool'? He really hoped so, because he had no clue what it meant otherwise. "I'll go change into them now," he said, forcing a smile as he took the bag and headed to Jackson's room.

Once he'd changed, Gregory stopped in front of the mirror and frowned. The clothing looked odd to him, but was this what 'normal' teenagers (or almost teenagers) wore?

Other than the clothes Deadlock gave him to wear to blend in to do his job, he'd always worn what he now realized were military-style clothing, plain shirts, cargo pants, and combat boots.

Jackson had called him a GI Joe, and Gregory almost punched him. He knew exactly what that meant, and in Deadlock being associated with the government like that was one of the greatest insults you could give someone.

Luckily, he'd paused long enough to realize the boy hadn't meant it as an insult, and he hadn't punched him for it.

Groaning, he rubbed his temples and took in a deep breath.

All his training didn't prepare him for actually living a normal life. It was only meant for him to blend in just long enough to take out his target. Half the things the Winfields talked about, he didn't have a clue.

Deadlock

Like he hadn't understood what the heck a missionary trip was before he'd asked them outright about it.

The Winfields talked about them quite a bit, and at first, Gregory had thought it was something like the missions the Deadlock operatives went on, but he soon realized they weren't.

Instead of being sent places to take a target out, or to ensure other parts of the organization were moving smoothly what they did on these missionary trips was 'help people' and spread the 'gospel', whatever that was.

It sounded like a waste of time and money to Gregory, but he never said it out loud. He was a hundred percent sure they wouldn't agree. The more time he spent with the Winfields, the more he realized how strange his life had been.

Shaking himself, Gregory quickly realized he'd been standing there, staring at the ground for several minutes. He needed to leave the room, or the Winfields would wonder what was taking him so long.

Out of habit, Gregory checked to make sure his clothing was in order before stepping out of the bedroom.

"What do you think?" he asked, moving to stand in the living room. He looked at Esther and waited. He honestly had no idea what she was going to say; apparently 'functional' wasn't something she looked for in clothing.

"They fit wonderful!" Esther said, clasping her hands together. "I'm so glad. I wasn't sure if we could afford to buy you new clothing on our budget, and you probably didn't want to wear Jonathan's clothing for the foreseeable future."

Gregory just shrugged. "I would have been fine with them," he said, and he meant it. Complaining was most definitely not something his father ever allowed from his men, or from his sons, no matter what it was about.

In fact, Gregory had seen him kill men for less.

Smiling, Esther stepped toward him, and it took all Gregory's self-control not to step back. "I'm sure you would have been," she said, bending down and kissing him on the forehead. "You're always so polite."

For only a fraction of a second, Gregory thought about telling her the reason. But again, that probably wasn't something normal. At least he was slowly starting to catch onto what he shouldn't share with them.

So instead of saying anything, Gregory just smiled and shrugged, a trick he'd quickly caught onto, whenever he wasn't sure how to respond.

"Well," Jonathan said, shoving himself off of the couch. "If this little fashion show is over, why don't we have dinner?" Mia and Jackson quickly agreed to that, and they all headed into the kitchen, where Jonathan and Esther threw something together while Gregory just watched.

He knew the Winfields would have found it strange, but he found their cooking fascinating They fried and grilled so much of the food they ate! It was nothing like the plain,

Deadlock

sometimes slightly warm food they ate at Deadlock.

They were just starting to make what they called 'crepes' when something through the kitchen window caught Gregory's eyes. Standing up straight from where he had been leaning against the counter, he glanced around and quickly realized no one else had seen anything.

But that didn't mean it hadn't been there.

Biting the inside of his lip, Gregory edged his way around the kitchen until he stood in front of the window. He twisted around, leaned against the counter, and looked out the window. He waited for a second, then he saw it.

A flicker of a shadow passed between two of the trees on the far side of the yard, and he could tell from the size that it was human. Turning away from the window, Gregory looked around the kitchen again and quickly realized that Jonathan and Esther were busy cooking, while Jackson and Mia were fighting.

None of them were paying any attention to him or what might be happening outside. With that thought, Gregory scooted toward the back door and silently slipped outside.

CHAPTER 12

Stepping out of the house, Gregory quickly noted how quiet it was. Even the irritating crickets weren't chirping. Wishing for his gun, but not wanting to have to slip back into the house to get it, Gregory jumped down the two steps into the grass.

Sweeping his gaze around the yard, Gregory couldn't see anything in the dark, but the trees surrounding him didn't help things. And the moonlight streaming down didn't help things by casting everything in shadows.

He couldn't see anything, and Gregory started to doubt himself. Maybe he'd imagined it; maybe it had just been a trick of the moonlight mixed with wind or something. *Sure… and maybe the Prime Minister of Bulgaria's death was an accident.*

Gregory moved toward the edge of the trees, looked around again, and was just about to turn around and head back into the house when a hand shot out from behind the nearest tree and grabbed his arm.

"Gregory, what are you doing?" Grew hissed, yanking

Deadlock

him behind the tree and out of sight of the house.

Sweeping his arm around, Gregory broke free from Grew's grip and shoved his brother back.

Gregory found himself instinctively moving into a self-defense stance. It was a good thing too because the next second Grew slammed into his chest and sent them both flying to the ground.

Automatically, Gregory wrapped his leg around Grew's. Then he pinned his brother's arm to his chest and quickly shoved him to the side and off-balance. The second he was on top, Gregory pinned his brother to the ground.

Grew tried to knee Gregory in the stomach, but Gregory quickly moved to the side, without letting him up. Gritting his teeth, he smacked Grew on the top of the head. "Grew, just stop it!" he hissed. "Or I'll make you regret it."

Glaring at him, Grew tried to punch him, but Gregory quickly pinned his arms to the ground before he could.

"I'm not afraid of you," Grew hissed, then he arched his back, pushed his knees up, and shoved Gregory off of him and onto the ground above his head. He followed through with the rest of the flip and landed on top of Gregory.

But before Grew could even pin him down, Gregory shoved him over, and they rolled to the side again. He hesitated for a second, then with a low growl, Gregory let his brother up and jumped to his feet. "I don't want you to be afraid of me."

Still glaring at him, Grew scrambled to his feet and

brushed the grass off of his shirt. "What are you doing, Greg?" he asked, his eyes searching Gregory's face as he began to circle him. "Why is the Preacher still alive? You were supposed to kill him, not…not whatever the heck you're doing! What *are* you doing? You're dressed like one of them, and I've been watching. What is your end game with them?"

"They're *normal,* Grew," Gregory whispered, ducking his head. "I'm sorry if for just a few weeks I want that too. Haven't you ever wanted that? Because I did, even before I saw what we were missing."

"Du hast den Verstand verloren!" Grew said under his breath, shaking his head at Gregory as his eyes narrowed. "What would Father say to any of this? Or Roman for that matter? They've trained us our whole lives to do our jobs, not… play house, or whatever this is you're doing here. Just do what you were sent here to do, and then we can both go home and act like this lapse in judgment never happened."

Gregory opened his mouth and worked his jaw, but no words came out. There was no way he could tell his brother he'd already decided that he wouldn't kill Jonathan, his target. It really was the truth; he understood that now.

The Winfields offered him something he'd never had. Even when their mother was alive they didn't have a normal family, and it was something he'd wanted for a very long time. Hesitating, Gregory took a step toward Grew. "You could stay here, you know," he said. "I could talk to the

Deadlock

Winfields about it."

Grew sneered at him and stepped back, his eyes flashing with anger. "No, if this is what you want…" He glanced toward the house and back to Gregory. "Then, fine! But don't expect me to give up my life because you've lost your mind! I hope you see sense before it's too late for you."

"I haven't lost my mind," Gregory said, fighting the urge to move closes, knowing that would only cause Grew to move back more. "Just… give me a little more time. I'll finish my testing and I'll come home." He knew it was a lie, even as the words left his mouth, but he could tell Grew would not hear that he wanted to stay.

"Fine," Grew whispered, his gaze dropping to the ground. "If you want to indulge yourself in this little rebellious streak of yours, go ahead. Just don't expect me to bail you out of this one."

So that's it huh? He thought Gregory was just being 'rebellious'? Didn't he want this as much as Gregory did? His frustration quickly came out as anger. "When have you ever bailed me out?!" he scoffed. "I think I would remember that."

Grew took a step forward and jabbed a finger out toward Gregory. "You have no idea what I've done for you!" he hissed. "You have no idea what it's like living in your shadow, never being good enough. Yet I never held that against you, and I never tried to outshine you or let anything make you look bad in front of Father." Then

Grew's voice dropped even lower. "Maybe I should have."

There was anger in his brother's voice that he'd never heard before. Maybe there was more going on than he'd thought. "Grew…" he started, trying to figure out what he should say, but he didn't have the chance before Grew spoke first.

"Have fun with your new *family*, Greg," he hissed, stepping back again. "It's obviously the one you would rather have. I miss her too." With that, he spun on his heel, and just as quickly as he'd appeared, he was gone.

Gregory buried his face in his hands and groaned. He'd never found it easy to talk to his brother, even before their mother died, but afterward it was much worse. It was as if she had been the last thread holding them together.

Why couldn't he see why he was doing this? Didn't he want to be normal as much as Gregory did? Gregory didn't know what to do. He could go after Grew, but what would he even say?

The hairs on the back of his neck stood up, and he knew someone was standing behind him. He had been so focused on Grew and trying to decide what to do, he hadn't even heard the person come up.

Glancing out of the corner of his eye, Gregory caught sight of Jonathan and inwardly sighed. Going after Grew wasn't an option anymore. Standing up a little straighter, Gregory decided to wait and see if the man would let him know he was standing there, and he did, by clearing his throat.

"Gregory, what are you doing out here?" Jonathan said, fighting a yawn as he pulled his jacket tighter around his shoulders.

Hesitating, Gregory turned toward him. He wasn't exactly sure how he was going to explain this. He knew for a fact that he was kind of a mess after wrestling with Grew on the slightly damp ground.

"You're a mess!" Jonathan said, his eyes growing wide. "What... what the heck happened to you?"

"Nothing, I just... tripped," Gregory said, and inwardly grimaced. *Tripped?* Was that really the best he could do? He'd been there only a short time, and he was already losing his edge. Before his testing, he could have lied at the drop of a hat... okay, maybe that phrase didn't exactly fit.

Gregory felt a little stupid when he had to fight back a laugh at the thought of having to come up with a lie if someone dropped a hat. He was pulled from that thought when he felt Jonathan's gaze still on him.

"You *tripped*?" Jonathan finally said, squinting at him. "Really?"

Well, it was too late to take the lie back, so he might as well go with it.

"Yeah," Gregory said. "I came out here to get a little air, and I tripped on that root over there. I didn't think I got that dirty."

Jonathan didn't look like he bought it, but he didn't

press the matter and just nodded. "Alright," he said, studying Gregory for a second longer. "Well, it's getting cold out here, so why don't you come back inside? Dinner's almost ready."

"Sure," Gregory said, shoving his hands into his pockets as he forced a smile, then followed Jonathan toward the house.

After only taking a couple of steps, Gregory stopped and glanced back toward the trees Grew had disappeared through and grimaced. In truth, Grew didn't even know what he was missing.

If only he'd tried a little bit more, maybe he could have talked Grew into leaving Deadlock too. But it was too late for that now.

CHAPTER 13

Gregory woke to find the Winfields all up very early, and he had no idea what was going on. Pulling a jacket on over his sweats and baggy t-shirt he wore for pajamas, he stepped out of the bedroom and found the family running around getting ready for something.

"What's going on?" Gregory said, glancing at his watch and realizing it was barely past six. For this family, that was unbelievably early to get up.

Esther turned toward him and smiled. "I was hoping you would get up," she said. "We'd like you to come with us to church that's what we're getting ready for. Speaking of... Mia, I found your shoes!"

"*Church?*" Gregory had heard the word before from his father after he heard his mother use it. If he remembered right, it was where a bunch of self-righteous people came together to talk about how horrible everyone else was, and how much better they were. It was hard to believe that these people went to something like that.

"Yes, church," Esther said, smiling at him. "So? Will you come with us?"

He couldn't say what his father had said about church, so he racked his brain for anything else he knew about the place, and he said that instead. "Um…Do I have to… wear a tie?" he asked. That hadn't been what he was going to ask, but it was probably a better idea than asking if he had to be a good person to go because he was pretty sure if that was the case, he wasn't getting in.

Esther laughed. "Not if you don't want to."

Gregory wasn't sure what to do, but he had a feeling saying no really wasn't the answer she wanted from him. So why not play along, at least for now? "Alright…." he asked. "I guess I'll go then."

"Wonderful!" Esther said, flashing him a smile as she hurried to take something out of the oven. "There's a suit hanging over there for you. We were hoping you would want to come, and that was one of the things Mrs. Kline gave us for you."

"Yes, ma'am," he said, stepping toward where the suit hung. He pulled it off and headed back to Jackson's room to change.

It didn't take him long to change. It wasn't the first time he'd worn a suit; his father had made sure they were as comfortable wearing them as anything else. Gregory hesitated a second before grabbing up the tie and slipping

Deadlock

it on. It only took him a second to remember how to tie it.

Once he was done, he headed back out of the room again and found Mrs. Winfield running around the kitchen, making breakfast, Gregory guessed. Biting his lip, he glanced around and cleared his throat. "Do you need help or something?"

"That's alright," she said, turning toward Gregory. "Oh! You look wonderful, but I thought you didn't want to wear a tie?"

Gregory shrugged. "Roman, my... um... Someone I used to know always said to 'look the part'. So I went with the tie," he said, tugging at it before he brushed it flat and stood up a little straighter.

Esther smiled at him. "Well, I think you look so handsome in it." She patted him on the cheek, before turning and handing him a bowl of cereal. "Why don't you join Jackson eating breakfast?"

With a nod, he took the bowl and headed into the dining room where Jackson was already eating. "So..." Gregory said, frowning as he leaned against the table, not bothering to sit down as he started to eat. "Do you go to... church every week?"

Jackson wiped the milk off his chin and nodded. "Yeah, since Daddy's the new pastor, we kind of have to go."

"Pastor..." Gregory mumbled under his breath. He studied the weird colors the cereal was leaving behind before looking over at Jackson again and tilting his head.

"Is that like a um… preacher?"

Chewing on his cereal, Jackson frowned. "I guess so," he said, shrugging. "There's lots of names for what he does. We better hurry, we've got to get going soon." With that, Jackson slurped down the last of his milk and scrambled to his feet.

"Right," Gregory said, then he opened his mouth and poured the cereal and milk into his mouth and swallowed. Knowing how to eat quickly was something else Deadlock made sure he knew.

Eating was important, so you could focus and do your job, but being able to eat quickly was even more important.

Once he was finished, he turned back to Jackson who was now staring at him. "What?" Gregory asked. "Is something wrong?"

"You just swallowed all of that… without choking? Don't let Mommy see you doing that," he said. "She doesn't like it when we eat too quickly."

"Well, I'm not going to tell her," Gregory said, placing the bowl onto the table as he turned toward the boy. "Are you?"

Jackson shook his head. "No, but you shouldn't do it," he said. "Mommy says eating too fast isn't good for you."

Gregory snorted. "I can think of a lot of things that are much worse," he mumbled under his breath. "Alright, I won't eat so fast anymore," he said, fighting the urge to roll his eyes as they headed out of the dining room.

Deadlock

A few minutes later, Gregory found himself waiting next to the front door, staring up at the roof and realizing how punctual his family had always been. If Father told them they were leaving at seven, they had better be ready at six forty-five.

Finally, Mr. and Mrs. Winfield hurried down the hallway with Mia and Jackson (who'd run off earlier, saying he'd forgotten something). Gregory shoved himself away from the wall he'd been leaning against and shoved his hands into his pockets.

"You guys ready to go?" he asked, biting his tongue to stop himself from saying anything else that might not have been as polite.

"Oh yes," Esther said, smiling as she glanced around. "Does everyone have everything they need?"

Gregory fought a groan as he ran his hand through his hair. What was there to need?

Besides a weapon (which he was pretty sure wasn't what she meant) Gregory couldn't think of a single other thing he needed. Did they know how to get ready *before* you needed to leave?

"Oh!" Mia cried. "I forgot the Gameboy for Alice!" With that, she spun around and bolted back down the hallway. Glancing toward the wall, Gregory momentarily wondered how many times he could hit his head against it before leaving a dent.

After what felt like a lifetime to Gregory, the Winfields

were ready to go and piled into their car. Taking the middle seat of the small car that they drove, Gregory popped the seatbelt on and quickly familiarized himself with everything. Including where the E-brake was, just in case.

As soon as everyone was inside the car and seated, Gregory rested his head back against the seat closing his eyes. And a moment later, he felt someone lean against him. His eyes flickering open, he glanced over and realized it was Mia.

Sighing, he shook his head and rested back against the seat. As long as she didn't start drooling, he'd leave her be until they got to the 'church', wherever that was. The next time he opened his eyes, the car had stopped next to an old white building with a strange tower at one end.

The four Winfields climbed out of the car, and Gregory hesitated a second before sliding out of the car and following them toward the door leading into the side of the weirdly shaped white building.

The smell of old wood and mildew hit Gregory as he stepped through the door, and he fought the urge to sneeze. *Man, how old is this place?* he wondered, looking around. *This was a church?* He wasn't sure what he was expecting, but Gregory had never been inside one before, and this place wasn't what he'd imagined.

All the buildings Deadlock used had been built after he was born. So not only were they newer, they looked nothing like this place. The door led into a hallway with a large

Deadlock

room at the end, with rows of benches with backs and slightly cushioned seats.

He continued to follow the Winfields toward the back row while looking around him and memorizing everything he saw. There were several exits, and Gregory quickly planned the fastest route out.

If he needed to make a fast escape, he would need to know exactly how to do that. For a second, Gregory paused and wondered what he was doing. Would there even be a reason for him to escape the church quickly?

Gregory hoped not, but out of habit, he allowed himself to work it out in his mind anyway. It wouldn't hurt to know it.

CHAPTER 14

Fidgeting in his seat, Gregory looked up at the dull wood roof. *Gosh, this is boring,* he thought, fighting the urge to hit his head against the back of the bench, repeatedly. So far all they'd done was sit there, while people slowly trickled in.

He didn't mind the fact that there weren't a ton of people watching him when he entered, but really? Did they have to get there so stinking early just to sit there?

Gregory was just dozing off when an alarm sounded in the back of his mind. He sat up straight and glanced around, trying to decide what had caused his body to tense. It didn't take him long to find the cause.

It was the FBI agent he'd met at the Winfields' a few days before. *What was his name? White!* Yes, it was Special Agent Benjamin White. What was he doing there?

His eyes followed the man as Agent White made his way to the back of the room, toward them. Glancing back and toward the nearest exit, Gregory grimaced and tried to decide if he should skip out before the agent got too close.

"Ben, this is a nice surprise," Esther said, standing to greet the agent. "What brings you here? Not that we're not glad to see you."

Gregory's heart skipped a beat as he waited for the answer. What *was* the FBI agent doing there? It was obvious that Esther hadn't been expecting him. Instinctively, Gregory's hand reached for the first weapon his eyes came upon.

The 'weapon' turned out to be a small piece of metal sticking out from behind the bench in front of him. From the looks of it, it was probably used as a spacer for the books sitting on the back of the bench.

"Are you here working?" Esther asked, and Gregory's head shot up. He highly doubted he'd like any 'work' the man was doing in that little town.

"Technically, I'm on vacation," Agent White answered. "I'm meeting a friend here. Well, friend and coworker. He's not on vacation though."

Great. So there was an active FBI agent in town. Gregory's brain barely registered the fact that the agent turned toward him as he tried to figure if he should still leave or not. Or maybe… maybe it was better if he just took the man out completely. Though, killing him in front of the church would complicate things.

It wasn't until the agent said his name that Gregory was pulled from his thoughts and looked toward him.

"Hello, Gregory," the agent said, flashing him a smile. "Nice to see you again."

Gregory blinked. "What?"

"I said it was nice to see you again," Agent White said, frowning as he tilted his head and studied Gregory. "Is everything all right?" he asked. "You look a little pale."

"Yeah," Gregory said, loosening his grip on the piece of metal as something loosened in his chest too. "Everything's fine. This is my natural complexion, though some ghosts have been jealous."

White cracked a smile and nodded. "Good," he said. "Though, I hope my friend doesn't hear that joke; he makes enough dumb ones all on his own."

Esther smiled. "Well, the service is about to start," she said. "So why don't we save our talking for later?"

Gregory glanced toward her, taking the cue of staying seated when she sat back down, though he wasn't exactly sure why she did that when just a couple of minutes later everyone stood up again.

They sang a bunch of weird, old-sounding songs (there were too many thous, thys, and thees in it for his liking), then they sat back down, and Gregory watched as everyone pulled out books as Jonathan moved toward the front of the Church.

Gregory noted that some of the books looked alike, but most of them didn't. Were they the same book? He didn't know much about books; most of the ones his father had

Deadlock

allowed them to read weren't probably books anyone here would know.

Shaking away those thoughts, Gregory ran his hand through his hair, feeling slightly awkward being the only person without a book on his lap.

Once at the front, Jonathan stepped behind a podium, then looked down at his own book and hesitated. Scanning the people in front of him, he frowned.

"Some of you know this, others don't," he said, clearing his throat as he rested against the podium. "But before moving here a couple of months ago, my family and I were living as missionaries in Mexico." He laughed. "I know, that might seem out of the blue for something I have to say, but maybe not."

Gregory wasn't quite sure why, but he found himself growing uncomfortable and scooted a little lower in his seat.

"There are bad people out there; we all know that. While there, my family worked to help the people affected by a cartel there. Those that know them know them by the name de los Muertos," Jonathan said, and Gregory was glad he didn't have a book on his lap because he was pretty sure he would have dropped it when he flinched at that name. "They were some of the worst people I've ever met."

He'd heard of them before; his father had mentioned them several times in fact. It was a common name in Deadlock while Gregory was growing up. In fact... they were critical to Deadlock's operations there in Mexico.

Slowly, the pieces of why his father had sent him there began to fall into place, and Gregory started to feel a little off. The Winfields obviously did much more in Mexico than they realized if they'd caught his father's attention.

Gregory looked up when he realized Jonathan was speaking again.

"Those men, and what they did… might have been horrible. But no matter what you've done, God still loves you," Jonathan said, and for a second, Gregory was sure he was looking at him. "No matter what's been done to you, or who you are, He knows you by name, and He knows everything about you. Yet, He still loves you and died so you could be forgiven for what you've done. God is willing to forgive you, if you're willing to repent and change your ways, but you have to ask him."

Glancing around, Gregory really looked at the other people sitting in the Church. They were all so… normal. And that, Gregory realized, was his problem. He wasn't normal. He came from a long line of men and women who worked in the shadows, controlling kingdoms and bringing their downfall.

God might be able to forgive the petty sins of these people, but Mr. Winfield had no idea what he'd done, or what he would have to do if he were ever to earn the respect of his father, though that was something he wasn't sure he wanted anymore.

Deadlock

One thing he did know was, he didn't belong here! Gregory gulped, and the next second, a pounding began in his ears. He quickly realized the pounding was his heart thudding in his chest.

Jonathan's voice had become just a buzz in the back of his head, but Gregory couldn't listen to it anymore. He needed air, and he needed it now! Forcing himself to keep his breathing under control, he put into motion the escape route he'd mapped out earlier when they'd just gotten there.

He slipped off the bench and dropped to the ground. Before Mrs. Winfield even had a chance to look over at him, Gregory rolled under his seat and hopped to his feet on the other side, before bolting out the nearest exit.

Shoving against the heavy door, Gregory stumbled out of the building and gulped in as much air as his lungs could handle. Then he moved to the side and rested against the wall. He could run five miles without running out of breath, but right then, leaning against the Church wall, he could barely breathe, and he didn't know why.

What was wrong with him?! Why were all of these stupid superstitions bothering him so much? Maybe he shouldn't be staying there anymore; the Winfields were obviously getting inside his head.

Gregory moaned. He wanted to hit something, but all he could do was kneel there clutching his head as he tried to gain control of himself again.

Using a breathing exercise he'd learned to do before going to the shooting range, Gregory tried to steady himself.

This was stupid! He was almost thirteen. He should have had better control of himself by now. He definitely shouldn't have run out of the church the way he did. Taking in another slow breath, Gregory straightened up and tugged at his suit.

Maybe he should go back in, but then again, he might have to explain why he'd left the way he did, and he wasn't sure he could. Gregory was still debating with himself when laughter brought his attention to the other side of the church.

Frowning, he took a step forward and followed the sound.

Chapter 15

When Gregory turned the corner, what he found was not what he was expecting. Five boys stood in a small cluster next to the church, spray painting the side of the building. Anger flared up in Gregory as he stepped toward them.

This place was obviously important to the Winfields, and he wasn't going to let them vandalize it like this. "Hey! Stop that," Gregory ordered, grabbing one of the boys by the arm and yanking him back.

The boy snorted and pulled his arm free from Gregory's easy grip. "What are you going to do about it? Stop us?" he asked, smirking.

Gregory shrugged as he looked the boys over, his mind already working out their strengths and weaknesses. "Yes," he said, his gaze moving back to the boy who was obviously the leader. "If I have to."

The boy shoved Gregory in the chest, and Gregory fell back a step. "That I'd like to see," the boy spat. "Come on, fight back!" With that, the boy shoved him again, slightly harder, but this time Gregory didn't move.

"Stop it," Gregory warned. Roman had warned him to never start a fight, but not to back down if one began. "Or you *will* regret it."

The boy laughed at that and glanced around at his pals. "Oh?" he said, smirking as he held out his arms. "What are you going to do about it? If it's a fight you want, then it's a fight you'll get." He shrugged off his jacket and tossed it to one of the other boys. "Let's do this, *church boy*."

Gregory sighed, loosening his tie. "There's one thing you should have known about me before you started this," he said, gritting his teeth as the boy swung at him, and he easily caught him by the wrist. "I'm not a 'church boy'."

In a flash, Gregory yanked the boy's wrist at an angle it wasn't supposed to go in, and he heard a quiet 'snap'. The boy yelled out in pain, clutching his now broken wrist as he stumbled back from Gregory and dropped to his knees. "Why did you do that?!"

"I did warn you, which was more than you deserved," Gregory said, straightening out his suit jacket. "But I'm guessing you've been breathing a little bit too deeply around the *paint* fumes."

"You're going to pay for this!" the boy snarled, cradling his arm.

Gregory couldn't help it, he laughed. He'd just broken the boy's wrist like it was a glow stick, and yet he was

Deadlock

threatening Gregory? Who wouldn't laugh at that? "Oh, is your daddy going to help you?" he asked, smirking at the boy.

The boy's eyes flashed with anger, and he glared at Gregory. "Get him!" he yelled at the other boys.

To Gregory's surprise, they actually listened. At least most of them did. Three boys sprang at him, but he just rolled his eyes. Keeping his hands resting against his jacket, Gregory easily sidestepped the first boy to reach him, kicking him in the back and sending him stumbling away as Gregory twisted around and dodged a punch from one of the others coming from the other side.

He quickly grabbed the boy's arm, twisted it around, and shoved him to his knees. Then he turned to face the last boy full on.

"Who taught you to fight? Your granny?" Gregory asked as the boy punched clumsily toward him.

Deflecting the punch, Gregory lunged toward him and caught him around the neck at the same time as he caught his arm, then he twisted around and brought the boy down, his body hitting against the ground with a 'thud'.

"That was a very bad idea," Gregory whispered, pinning the boy down with his knee. "Since this fight wasn't originally your idea, I'll give you the courtesy of asking you, which of your bones would you like me to break first?"

"Get away from him!"

Gregory gritted his teeth at the sound of the other boy's

voice, just before he plowed into Gregory and sent them both flying to the ground. Gregory rolled over and out from under him and was on him in a second.

Shoving his knee against the boy's chest, Gregory's hands quickly found the boy's neck, and he wrapped them tightly around it.

The boy gasped for breath and grabbed at Gregory's arms, but there was no way the scrawny kid could break his grip, and with a little more pressure, Gregory could choke the air completely from the boy's lungs. Already, Gregory could tell the boy was losing consciousness.

If it went as Roman always said, the boy would be dead within seconds. He heard footsteps moving toward him but paid them no mind. His mind focused on one thing and one thing only, ending the boy.

"Gregory, stop!" Jonathan yelled from somewhere behind him. Gregory heard Jonathan, but his words didn't register. Like he always did when he was in the middle of a fight, Gregory had just gone into overdrive.

That's why when he felt someone touch his arm, he reacted instinctively.

Moving quickly, Gregory twisted around, stepping his leg around and slamming it against his attacker. He pivoted around and brought them to the ground. The next second, he had the person pinned to the ground, with his legs wrapped tightly around their neck.

It took Gregory a second to realize what he was doing,

but luckily for him and Jonathan, he did realize, before he cut the man's oxygen off completely. Swallowing, Gregory released him and quickly jumped to his feet.

He moved back when he realized Jonathan hadn't come out alone, and the rest of the Winfield family was there too. "Are you alright?" Esther asked, kneeling beside her husband as she glanced toward Gregory, and he quickly ducked his head.

With his head still down, Gregory glanced around and saw the other boys had scurried off. Well, most of them had. The boy he'd been on top of when Jonathan came out was still lying on his back, and the boy whose wrist he'd broken was still seething next to the wall, glaring at Gregory.

"I'm fine," Jonathan said, slowly shoving himself up off the ground. "I don't think I broke anything either. Which, with the force he hit me onto the ground with, is surprising. *And* how hard he kicked me."

Gregory felt the heat rush to his face as he felt something he'd never felt before.

Guilt.

He hated himself for that. He had been sent to kill this man, and now he felt guilty about hurting him? Had he completely lost his mind? Looking at the Winfields' faces, he quickly realized they all had very different expressions.

Mrs. Winfield was shocked, while Mr. Winfield's gaze was calculating. And both the kids? Well, they both stood there staring at Gregory, with their jaws hanging open. But the worst part of all was the group of people standing behind them, who Gregory recognized as people from inside the Church.

Being the center of attention was a horrible place for a Deadlock to be, but at the moment he didn't have much choice.

Instead of dwelling on that though, Gregory stood up straight, clasped his hands behind his back, and looked straight ahead. "Mr. Winfield, where would you like me to go?" he asked, not even looking over at the man.

Jonathan seemed to hesitate, still studying Gregory. "Why don't you get in the car," he said, motioning across the parking lot to where their small car still sat. "We'll talk about this later."

Without giving any verbal response, Gregory gave him a sharp nod and did as he was told. Stepping back, he twisted around to face the other direction and marched toward the waiting car.

Once he was blocked from view by one of the larger cars, Gregory stopped and took in a slow breath. What was wrong with him? He shouldn't feel guilty, especially because he'd hurt the man he was sent there to kill.

It was the dumbest thing he could do. If his father was there… well, Grew wouldn't be wanting him to come back to Deadlock. He would be a disgrace to his family and a dishonor to the Deadlock name.

Shaking himself, Gregory started toward the car again.

Deadlock

Maybe it wasn't quite as much guilt he was feeling as it was regret, knowing the Winfields wouldn't want him to stay with them after this.

For a short time, he'd allowed himself to believe he might have found a place where he could just be him, and not wonder every moment if he was doing things right. Or if someone would be disappointed in him, whether his father or Roman.

None of that mattered now though. It was obvious the Winfields were disappointed in him.

Maybe that was just who he was. Maybe he'd never find a place where he could do something right for more than a couple of minutes. Maybe he would always be a disappointment to those who knew him.

Chapter 16

Sweeping around, Gregory kicked the nearest tire. Why was he so stupid to even try? He'd learned enough about the Winfields to know that if they ever found out who he really was, he would get a one-way ticket to the fancy new prison they'd built in Colorado. What did they call it? ADX Florence? Yeah, he was pretty sure that was the name, though he didn't want to find out for sure.

He was just thinking about kicking the air out of the tire he was still standing next to when Gregory saw movement out of the corner of his eye.

Slowly, so as not to draw attention to the fact that he was looking, Gregory turned in that direction and spotted a boy strolling away from the end of the church and toward a car that had just pulled into the parking lot.

Gregory quickly realized it was one of the smarter boys from the fight earlier. Well, Gregory was 89.2% sure he hadn't been one of the ones he fought, but then again, it was already kind of a blur, and he wasn't positive.

Deadlock

Yet, he was still there, and he didn't look dirty or beat up at all.

Something about what was happening was off, but Gregory couldn't put his figure on it. Until the driver of the black sedan rolled down his window and pulled off his sunglasses, and a strange feeling entered Gregory's stomach. There was something familiar about him, but he couldn't quite figure out why.

He knew he'd never seen the man before in his life.

So instead of doing anything to get involved, Gregory watched as the boy spoke to the man, then motioned to the church, and the man nodded and climbed out of the car. They spoke again and the boy grew a little bit more adamant, but not much.

It didn't take a genius to figure out that they were now talking about the fight. That's why Gregory ducked down and hid behind the vehicle he'd kicked earlier. Looking through the windows of the vehicle, Gregory could see them both scanning the parking lot, and the boy shook his head and shrugged.

Gregory stayed low and watched as they shook hands and the man went through the back door of the church, while the boy took a backpack out of the back of the vehicle and vanished down the street.

It was obvious they knew each other quite well. But who were they? And what was the man doing inside the church? Gregory thought about going back to the Winfields and telling them, but they had sent him to the car. And when he looked down at himself, Gregory realized he was covered in dirt.

With a grimace at the thought that Mrs. Winfield wasn't going to be happy about that, Gregory felt like kicking himself this time. Why did he even care what they thought? It *shouldn't* matter to him, but for some stupid reason, it did.

He shoved himself away from the stranger's vehicle and started toward the Winfields' again.

When he finally arrived at the Winfields' car, Gregory tried the door and realized with a sigh that it was locked. Which wouldn't have been too bad if he'd had a metal hanger on him, but that wasn't exactly something he carried around with him.

That didn't mean he couldn't find another way into the car.

Patting his pockets down, Gregory quickly found the piece of metal he'd forgotten he'd put in his pocket, and that gave Gregory an idea. He was glad Mrs. Winfield hadn't given him any dress shoes to wear as he bent down and began to undo the lace of his left combat boot.

Once he had it free, he stood back up and moved toward the car door.

Keeping the lace in one hand, Gregory fished the piece of metal out of his pocket and worked it between the seal of the door and the car itself. Once he had it far enough in, Gregory took the shoelace, looped it, and carefully lowered the lace through the small space the piece of metal gave him.

After a bit of maneuvering, Gregory got the lace around the metal piece. With one hand on the top holding one end of the shoelace, and the other hand holding the lace at the end of the glass, Gregory carefully hooked the lace around the little lock sticking out from the bottom of the window.

Once the lace was hooked around it, Gregory pulled on both ends until the loop tightened around the lock. Then with a tug, the lock came up and there was a 'click' as the door unlocked.

Gregory opened the door, hit the 'unlock' button, and climbed into the back seat. He was just making himself comfortable when he heard footsteps and glanced out the back window of the car.

It was the Winfields.

Sighing, Gregory turned back again and stared out the front window as Jonathan opened the driver door, frowning. "After sending you out here, I thought I remembered locking it," he said. "I thought you'd be waiting outside, or come back."

"It wasn't locked," was all Gregory said as he crossed his arms, closed his eyes, and leaned his head back against the seat. He was glad his obvious body language worked, and neither of the Winfield parents said anything else to him as they climbed in, and they headed back to *their* home.

Even after picking up lunch and eating it, Jackson and

Mia were both quiet on the way back to the house, and for that Gregory was grateful. He was not in a talking mood, especially with a couple of sheltered children who knew nothing about the real world. The world Gregory came from, the one he would have to go back to soon.

Once they reached the front of the house and stopped, it took quite a bit of his self-control not to shove either Jackson or Mia out of his way so he could get out.

He hadn't spoken a word since they'd left the church parking lot, and even as they entered the house, Gregory remained silent. He was just waiting for the punishment they were sure to inflict.

Silently he stayed in the corner of the living room, where no one seemed to notice him, while Mr. and Mrs. Winfield ushered Mia and Jackson upstairs to change before they got their clothing dirty. Like Gregory had already done to his.

Maybe it was because they were used to loud children, but once their two kids were gone, they didn't act like they realized Gregory was still there. His supposition was confirmed when they started talking about him.

"Did you see the way he fought those boys? Most of them were much bigger than him," Esther whispered, moving closer to her husband as Gregory continued to just stand there and watch. "Yet, he knew exactly what he was doing, and he *actually* fought off four boys at one time!"

"He did," Jonathan agreed, nodding his head as he

Deadlock

rolled out his shoulder. "I also *felt* it when he tossed me on the ground like it was nothing. I did not expect that kind of a reaction out of him."

"I didn't realize it was you," Gregory said, stepping toward them. *Might as well get this over with*, he thought, inwardly sighing.

Esther spun around and nearly hit Gregory. "Oh! Gregory," she said, placing her hand over her heart. "I didn't realize you were standing there."

"I didn't figure I was allowed to be anywhere else," Gregory said, looking straight ahead as he clasped his hands behind his back and waited for the inevitable.

"Sit down," Jonathan said, motioning to the couch in front of them as he rubbed his back. "You're acting like you're about to be executed." Gregory knew he was joking, but he didn't find it particularly funny.

But instead of saying that, Gregory just gave them a sharp nod, took a step back and sat down. Esther sat down, and with a lot of groaning, Jonathan sat down on the other couch beside her.

It was then Gregory realized maybe he *had* thrown him onto the ground a little bit harder than the man would have expected if he'd expected it at all. Which he wasn't sure he had, and that was strange for Gregory to think about.

In any situation, he was ready for a fight. Which, he supposed, was part of the problem.

Esther sighed and glanced toward her husband as she

gripped his hand, and Jonathan turned his gaze toward Gregory. "Do you know why we want to talk to you?" he asked.

Here we go again, Gregory thought. *Another interrogation.* Well, as Roman taught him, he should tell them the truth when it would not harm himself or Deadlock. So that was what he would do.

"No, sir," Gregory said, shifting to look the man full in the face. "I don't know why you want to talk to me."

Esther sighed. "You really don't know?" she asked, her voice soft and so much like his mother's.

"I really don't," Gregory said, swallowing as he shook the memory of his mother away. "But I can make my guesses. I'm sorry I hurt you, and I'm sorry I got this suit dirty. But you seemed to be upset about something other than that, and I'm not quite sure what it is. So please, enlighten me."

"We want to talk to you about your fight with those boys outside of church," Jonathan said, and Gregory could tell he was trying to keep his voice level. "I don't know if you're aware of this, but you sent a couple of those boys to the hospital. If we hadn't found you when we did, you could have killed that one boy!"

Good, Gregory thought, but decided against saying it out loud. Instead, he opted for just sitting there in silence and staring out the window behind them. Watching the trees outside swaying back and forth was *very* entertaining, if he

Deadlock

was a cat.

Gregory had a feeling this was going to be a long 'chat'.

CHAPTER 17

Jonathan sighed, shoved himself off the couch, and moved to sit beside Gregory. Gregory stiffened, but didn't move. "If all we ever do is repay violence with more violence, what good are we doing?" Jonathan asked, bending forward and trying to force Gregory to look at him.

Gregory gritted his teeth and turned toward him. "They were vandalizing your building," he said, slowly. He felt like he was talking to a child. "And it was obvious to me that they needed to be put in line."

"That wasn't your place," Esther said. "You should have come in and told one of us. You shouldn't have gotten involved yourself."

He couldn't believe how naive they were! "Is that really what you think I should have done?" he asked, looking from her to Jonathan.

Slowly, they both nodded. "Yes," Jonathan said. "That's what we think you should have done.

"Dann seid ihr einen Menge Idioten!" (Then you are a

bunch of idiots!) Gregory spat, jumping to his feet as he threw his hands up. "If I'd gone back inside, they would have either just continued at it or left before you could catch them."

"Was that… Danish?" Esther asked, blinking.

"What? No!" Gregory groaned and ran his hand through his hair. Not only did she mistake his words, but she also didn't even get the right language out of it. His statement rang truer with every second.

"Can't you tell the difference between German and Danish?" Gregory asked, squinting at her. "I'm aware they sound slightly alike, but seriously! Other than the *Danish*, who would learn Danish? It's a useless language for us to use."

"Us?" Esther asked, raising an eyebrow.

Gregory barely flinched, though he quickly realized his slip up. "Yes, 'us'," he said, rolling his eyes. "Humans. But I think we might be getting sidetracked."

"You're right," Jonathan said, standing and moving to stand in front of Gregory and look down at him. "What happened to you? When we came out there, you… you were in some kind of trance. You barely even seemed to realize it was me until you threw me to the ground and wrapped your legs around my neck. Did you even know what you were doing?"

Gregory knew what they were talking about, but it wasn't a trance, it was just the way he dealt with fighting. It was the only way he was able to do some of the things Deadlock expected of him.

His father had always told him it would get easier with time and experience, but so far, that wasn't the case. So he just didn't think about what he was doing. "What's my punishment?" Gregory finally said, instead of answering the man's question.

Jonathan frowned. "What?"

"I know you're going to punish me," Gregory said, crossing his arms and looking up at Jonathan as he shoved his chin out. "I would just like to know what it is and get it over with if you don't mind."

Jonathan glanced toward Esther. "Alright," he said, crossing his arms too. "In that case, what do you think your punishment should be?"

"I don't know," Gregory said, frowning. "I've never picked my punishments. It's not exactly part of my job. I assume it's yours?" He was pretty sure that was one of the few things his family had done normally, at least that's what he'd thought spending the last several days with the Winfields. Maybe he was wrong?

"How would your father punish you?" Esther asked, standing and moving to Jonathan's side before grabbing his hand as she turned back toward Gregory.

Gregory blinked, then fought back a laugh. "Honestly? I wouldn't be punished for something like this." Ironically, Gregory realized his father would probably have been

Deadlock

proud of him. He hadn't backed down, even when he was outnumbered.

Though the reason he'd faced off with the boys probably wouldn't have made him happy.

Clearing his throat, Jonathan nodded. "But if he were to punish you?" he asked. "What would he do?"

Gregory didn't understand why they cared, but he didn't see a problem in telling them the truth. "A light punishment would probably be something like, one week without any food," he said, shrugging as he looked from one of them to the other. "And sometimes extra training from Roman." The worst was when the punishments were put together.

Spending all day getting beat up with an empty stomach wasn't exactly what Gregory would call fun.

Looking over at Esther, Gregory realized he had said something wrong. She looked horrified. He glanced toward Jonathan and realized that the man looked strange as well. But before he could ask them what he'd said wrong, the phone sitting on the table at the end of the couch rang out loudly.

Sighing, Esther quickly rose to her feet and hurried to answer it. "Hello, Winfields," she said. "Esther speaking." There was a long pause, and Esther grimaced, glancing toward Jonathan. "Yes, Mrs. Galister," she said, sighing. "He does live with us, and yes, we are taking care of the situation. Alright, I'll make sure he knows that. Yes ma'am.

Tell your sister we're sorry, and we are going to punish him. Now, I don't think that's quite necessary!" She huffed. "Goodbye."

Once she was finished, Jonathan cleared his throat. "Who was that?"

"That was the aunt of the boy Gregory choked," Esther said, after placing the phone back in its holder and turning toward Gregory. "She just called to yell at me, and I doubt it will be the last call we'll get today."

Jonathan grimaced. "Besides yell, what else did she have to say?"

Esther dropped her gaze to the ground and clasped her hands, placing them on her lap. "Well… she made it quite clear that she expects us to punish Gregory," she said. "She had some… colorful ideas."

"Well, you can tell her, and anyone else that calls, I won't be bothering any of you anymore," Gregory said, stepping away from them. "I really shouldn't have stayed here as long as I have." With a grimace, Gregory realized that even if he left now, there was no way he would be able to finish his mission.

"Now wait a second, Gregory," Jonathan said, stepping toward him.

"What for? For you to yell at me some more?" Gregory asked, not a hint of anger in his voice. It was just a question to him, but they both looked hurt by his words. "I get it, you obviously think I did something wrong. I don't really know

Deadlock

what it was, but I guess that doesn't matter. I'll go change back into my clothes, then I'll go and we can all act like this never happened." *Except for the fact that I probably don't have anywhere to go back to now.* Maybe there was a tiny chance his father would let him back into Deadlock without killing Jonathan, but it would probably mean someone else would do it instead.

"Gregory, we need to talk before any of us does anything crazy," Jonathan said, holding out his hands as Esther rose to her feet and moved to stand beside him.

Sighing, Gregory let his shoulders droop as he ran his hand through his hair. "Do you want to punish me before I go?" he asked, glancing up at them. "Is that what this is about? Because if that is…"

"No," Jonathan said, cutting him off as he shook his head and took a step closer to Gregory. "That's not what I wanted to say."

Gregory squinted at him. "Then what?"

Jonathan sighed and gave Gregory a small smile. "Why did you leave in the middle of the service today?"

CHAPTER 18

Gregory stared at the man. Why did he leave in the middle of the service today? That was not what he'd been expecting him to ask. "What?" Gregory said, feeling stupid as soon as he said it. He should have easily come up with *something* else to say, instead of a one-syllable word.

Jonathan glanced toward Esther again and took a step closer to Gregory, ducking his head down so he was closer to Gregory's height. "Why'd you leave church?" he asked softly as he placed a hand on Gregory's shoulder.

He wasn't quite sure why, but Gregory felt heat rush to his face, and he quickly ducked his head. "I... I don't know," he mumbled, shoving his hands into his pockets as he took in a breath for five seconds, before holding it and letting it out again.

"Gregory," Jonathan whispered, bending down to catch his eye. "Do you... do you know God?"

"No," Gregory said, without hesitating as he stood up and held his chin up high. "Trust me, he's never wanted anything to do with me either. So why should I want anything to do with him? I only went to that church as a courtesy to you." He glanced toward Esther. "I went and I stopped those boys from defacing the side of your building as my way of repaying you. I don't plan on going again, and I'm sorry if helping you out wasn't something you wanted me to do."

Esther slowly moved toward him too. "Gregory, you don't have to repay us," she said. "That's not why we did it."

"Yes, I do." *A Deadlock doesn't owe a debt to anyone.* "And if this God of yours really cared about me..." He bit his tongue and shook his head. "Then why did he take my mother and leave me with my father? Couldn't he have at least taken them both?" He sucked in a breath much quicker this time as he forced himself to hold it for five seconds, before continuing at a normal tone. "You think my family's a cult, which I understand is a bad thing in your eyes. But my mother wasn't a part of that; she wasn't a part of what my father... had us do. So why did your God let her die and let my father live? Trust me, he doesn't deserve it! *She* did."

Gregory stopped himself from saying any more, knowing if he did, he might not be able to control his emotions anymore. And he *needed* to keep his emotions in check.

But more than that, he needed the time to realize what he'd just said. He hadn't meant to say any of it, yet he'd meant every word.

He never would have admitted it while he was still a part of Deadlock, but he hated his father. For what he'd done and what Gregory knew he was going to do. The man was a monster; he'd known that even before meeting the Winfields.

He hadn't really cared about Gregory and Grew, as long as they were good little soldiers and always did what they were told. Well, Gregory was done with that.

"Gregory," Esther started again, but Gregory held up a hand and stopped her.

"You want to know if I know this God of yours?" Gregory asked. "No, not really. But I heard enough today to know that I'm not on his top list for Heaven!" He yanked his arm away from Jonathan and took a couple of steps back. "But do you know what? I'm not sure I care. Would the other place be much worse than what I've already been through?"

"Gregory, that's not true!" Jonathan said, reaching out to him, but stopping himself when he seemed to realize Gregory didn't want that. "God loves you, Gregory. He knows everything about you, and He still loves you."

Loves me? Gregory almost laughed. If their God really knew him, then he wouldn't love him. His own father didn't love him, why would an almighty deity? Especially if they really did know everything about him?

"Give me my punishment already!" Gregory said,

throwing up his hands. "I'll take *anything* over this conversation."

Esther flinched. "Gregory, we just care about you," she said. "That's all."

"You shouldn't," he whispered, stepping back. It would do them no good if they actually cared about him. In fact, it would make things that much worse. People who cared were the ones who were hurt the worst. "Please, just tell me my punishment."

"Well, we'll have to talk it over," Jonathan said, glancing toward Esther as he bit his lip and turned back toward Gregory. "How about, for now, you skip dinner and go to bed. Does that sound fair?"

"Yeah, whatever," Gregory said, shrugging as he ducked his head and stepped back again. "I'll go now then." With that, he spun around and split out of the living room, up the stairs, and into Jackson's room.

Closing the door behind him, Gregory moved toward the bunkbed and rested his forehead against one of the posts. He'd been a fool to think he could stay here. He should have known he wouldn't be able to fit in.

Maybe… maybe if he talked to Grew, he would be willing to help him get back into their father's good graces. If he couldn't go back to Deadlock… he wasn't sure where he'd go. But with his training, it probably wouldn't be that hard for him to find work.

Sighing, he shoved himself away from the bunkbed and

looked around him.

Either way, he couldn't stay here anymore. But if he was going to survive on his own, it would probably be best if he took a couple of things with him, clothing included. *Speaking of…* Gregory thought, looking down at himself. It would probably be best if he changed out of the suit before leaving.

Pulling off the suit jacket, Gregory quickly changed into a pair of sweatpants, a T-shirt, and an old sports jacket. Once changed, he looked around the messy room (well, messy by his father's rules) and quickly spotted a backpack sticking out from under Jackson's bed.

It would probably be best if he took that with everything he needed in it.

Bending down, he grabbed the strap and yanked the empty backpack out. As he picked it up, a book fell out and thudded onto the ground. Flinching, he looked over at the room and was grateful no one seemed to have heard him.

He picked the book up and flipped it over. Across the cover, it read, 'Children's Bible'. "Bible?" he mumbled, frowning. Wasn't that the name on all the books everyone was looking at during church?

Biting his lip, he flipped it open and skimmed through it. Then toward the end, he stopped and looked down at the illustration. What he saw caused Gregory to grimace at the picture. This was in a kid's book?

It was a picture of a man, hanging from a post. Blood on

his hands and feet, with what looked like a Roman soldier getting ready to stab him with a sword in the side. Gregory's father had taught him enough about torturing people that he knew that kind of death would have been very painful.

If this was what the Winfields read to their children, maybe they weren't all that different from his own family. Shaking away those thoughts, Gregory closed the book again and shoved it back under the bed.

Shaking away any thought of the book, Gregory set to work picking out the bare necessities from Jackson's closet, and the clothing they'd given him. He'd need to grab non-perishable food out of the Winfields' pantry, but that would have to wait until later, once everyone was asleep.

By the time Jackson was sent to bed, Gregory had all his things packed up, folded nicely, and placed into the backpack sitting tucked on the corner of the top bunk.

Gregory himself lay fully dressed under the sheets, his eyes closed and his chest rising and falling slowly while Jonathan and Esther said goodnight to Jackson, kissing and tucking him into bed. Something Gregory vaguely remembered his mother doing before she died. He wasn't even sure his father had ever even been in his room, or Grew's.

He waited almost an hour until he was a hundred percent sure that Jackson was sound asleep. Then, moving quietly, he slid down the ladder and landed softly onto the carpeted ground.

Once standing, he pulled the backpack over his shoulder and headed toward the door. Halfway there, he stopped and glanced back one last time, wondering if he should take the gun with him.

But after everything that had happened since he came here, he didn't trust himself with it anymore. He didn't know what he would do. Would he be able to use it anymore? Or had he gone completely soft and useless?

If he took the gun and couldn't use it, then it was useless to him and would only serve to give someone a weapon to use against him. Still, it wasn't an easy thing for him to do. At least he still had the steak knife he'd taken the first day he was there, hidden among the clothing in his backpack.

Tightening his grip on the backpack strap, Gregory slipped out into the hallway and hurried down the steps, careful to avoid the third, sixth, and tenth, which he knew squeaked loudly under the lightest of weight.

He reached the bottom and headed through the kitchen and into the pantry, where he quickly filled up the rest of his backpack with the lightest things he could find that would serve for his meals the next several days.

Zipping the backpack up again, he pulled it onto his back and headed toward the door leading out of the kitchen and into the yard. He was just wrapping his hand around the handle when he heard the floor on the other side of the room groan.

"Gregory?" he heard Jonathan say behind him. "What are you doing?"

CHAPTER 19

Gregory's shoulders sagged as he slowly turned toward Mr. Winfield. "What does it look like I'm doing?" he asked, sighing. "I'm leaving." He shrugged. "I would have thought that was obvious."

The man flinched and ducked his head. "Gregory, look..." Jonathan sighed. "What we said earlier, this wasn't what we wanted. We're just... we're just trying to figure out this whole thing with... your past. Now come on, give me your backpack and we can talk about this."

Shaking his head, Gregory gripped the strap over his left shoulder. "I thought this would make you happy," he said. "It's obvious to me that I don't belong here, and... I don't think I'll ever fully fit in with you people."

"'You people'?" Jonathan repeated, squinting at him. "Gregory, what does that even mean?"

"Oh, come on!" Gregory scoffed. "You might be normal, but I'm pretty sure you're not that stupid. You know exactly what that's supposed to mean. I don't think the same way as you guys do. If I did what I really wanted to do, those boys would have gone away much worse than they did."

Jonathan grimaced. "You're right, we wouldn't have wanted that. And sure, we were upset about the fight outside of church. But that doesn't mean we want you to leave."

Gregory snorted. "You don't really want me around, not if you really knew what I've done," he said, shaking his head as he thought about just leaving. After how easy it had been to put the man onto the ground at the church, he doubted the man would be able to stop him, assuming he wanted to. "You're all so... normal, and... innocent. I doubt you've done a bad thing in your life."

"We're not perfect either," Jonathan said, moving closer to Gregory. "I've done things I shouldn't have too."

"What? Did you steal a Gerber LST when you were little?" Gregory scoffed.

Jonathan blinked and looked confused. "Baby food?" he said, frowning. "Is that what you're talking about?"

Sighing, Gregory ran his hand through his hair. "Why would I be talking about baby food?" he whispered, shaking his head. "The fact that you think that's what I'm talking about is my point exactly."

Jonathan grimaced and bent down so he was at eye level with Gregory. "Well, God knows exactly what you've done, and he still loves you. He loved you so much that he *died* for you," he said, tapping Gregory's chest. "He would have done it if you were the only person on earth."

A memory flickered through Gregory's mind, of a story his mother told him when he was little. That's when he realized he knew who the man in the kids' book was supposed to be. "Jesus," he said, flinching at the way that sounded as he looked up at the man. "That's who you're talking about, isn't it?"

Jonathan stood up and blinked down at Gregory. "Oh… So you know who Jesus is?" he asked, crossing his arms. Gregory rolled his eyes at the man's obvious attempt at covering up his surprise.

"Yeah, I just… my mom used to tell me stories about him," Gregory said, pinching the bridge of his nose. "But… no! Those were stories my mother used to make up to get me and… us to sleep. He… he wasn't real, just a hero she made up to make me feel better."

"Did she?" Jonathan asked, squeezing Gregory's shoulder. "A man who was willing to die for those that didn't deserve it? Taking their death upon Himself, and sacrificing Himself for those who owed Him everything?"

Gregory squirmed and tried to get his thoughts back into a straight line. Because what Jonathan said was right, and they weren't exactly just vague terms he was using like a fortuneteller would 'see' the future.

Because he was spot on, Gregory would know; he still remembered the day his mother told him that story. He was only four at the time, but he'd cried for an hour afterward.

Deadlock

Even now, after all these years, he still couldn't understand why someone would die for someone else like that. Someone who obviously didn't deserve it.

Swallowing, Gregory looked up at Jonathan again. "You think that story's true?" he whispered. "You think your God died like that?"

"He's not my God, Gregory," Jonathan said, shaking his head as he smiled at him. "He's just *God.* And yes, I do believe that's what He did. He loved us *so* much that He was willing to die for us. Not because we deserved it, but because He cared about us that much. We're His children, and He loves us."

His head spinning, Gregory rubbed at his eyes. *No!* What he'd done was bad enough, but what would his father think if he started to believe those fairytales his mother used to tell him and Grew?

Slowly, Gregory shook his head. "Just because we're 'His children' doesn't mean he loves us!" he hissed. "Family doesn't always work that way. Sometimes fathers don't love their children; I should know!"

Gregory knew he shouldn't have said it the second the words had left his mouth, but by then it was too late. Jonathan sighed and knelt in front of him. *Doesn't he know how dangerous a position that is?* Gregory wondered, then he realized that he probably didn't. The Winfields didn't seem to know those kinds of things.

"Gregory," Jonathan said softly as he placed his hand on

Gregory's arm again. "Just because you came… from a bad home, doesn't mean that we care about you less, or that God doesn't love you."

That was it. Gregory couldn't take this anymore!

"Stop it! Just stop it! I'm not who you think I am!" Gregory yelled, throwing up his hands and clutching his head as he took a step back. "Whatever you think you know about my past, I can promise you that it's not the truth."

"What is that supposed to mean?" Jonathan asked, slowly rising back to his feet. "Gregory?"

But Gregory ignored him as he squeezed his eyes shut and took in a deep breath. He didn't mean to lose it like that. He'd *never* lost it like that before. If his father had been there… Well, he wouldn't have reacted the same way as Jonathan.

And that fact seemed to make it worse.

"Don't," Gregory said when Jonathan reached out toward him. He took another step back from the man, his back pressing against the door. It was his only escape, but he realized now, he couldn't take it.

But he wasn't going to be a coward about this.

"You want to know what it means? I have one word for you to tell your FBI friend," Gregory said, standing up a little straighter as he looked Jonathan straight in the eye. "More accurately, a name for him."

Gregory swallowed and pulled his shoulders back

"Deadlock. Ask him what he knows about Deadlock,

then you'll understand what I mean. You wanted to know where I came from? Well, you're going to find out, and don't blame *me* when you don't care about me afterward."

Jonathan studied him for a long moment. "Alright, I'll ask him," he said, giving him a small smile. "But you're going to stay here with us until we do. Okay? We're not going to let you slip away that easily."

Gregory knew it was stupid. Once they found out who he was, they wouldn't want him there anymore, and he would (at the very least) end up in a juvenile detention center. But still… he didn't really want to go.

"Alright," he whispered, sighing as he lowered his backpack off of his shoulder. "I'll stay, for now."

Jonathan smiled. "Good! So how about we go back to bed, huh?" he asked, wrapping his arm around Gregory's shoulder and tugging him toward the stairs.

For a split second, Gregory's instincts wanted him to grab the man's arm and throw him to the ground, but luckily he was able to fight the urge, and instead, slowly made his way to the stairs.

"Goodnight, Mr. Winfield," Gregory said, shrugging off Jonathan's arm from around his shoulders.

"Goodnight, Gregory," he said. Then without warning, Jonathan bent down and kissed Gregory on the forehead.

Gregory jumped back and grimaced. "What was that?!" he cried, rubbing the spot as hard as he could.

"It was a kiss goodnight," Jonathan said, chuckling as he

grinned down at Gregory. "I torture both Mia and Jackson with it too, every night. So you'd better get used to it because I'm going to do it to you too."

Gregory squinted at him. It was the strangest torture method he'd ever heard of but wasn't completely unbelievable. "Fine," he huffed. "Whatever." Shaking his head, he hurried up the stairs and quietly back into Jackson's room, before he slipped into bed.

CHAPTER 20

No! Gregory sat up so quickly, he almost hit his head against the roof. Breathing heavily, it only took him a second to realize it had been a dream. Once he did, he squeezed his eyes shut and dropped his head back against the pillow again.

He hated this! Why were the nightmares back again? Gregory wondered. He hadn't had a single one since coming to the Winfields, and that was the longest he'd gone since his mother died.

But now that he thought about it, these weren't the same kind of nightmares. This time, it hadn't been about his mother.

No, this time it was the Winfields who died, and Gregory didn't know why that bothered him so much. He barely knew them! Rolling over, he muffled a moan in his pillow. What was wrong with him?

Get yourself under control, Gregory ordered himself as he took in a deep breath, while in the back of his mind he heard the sound of someone climbing up the ladder.

"Greggy," Jackson whispered, tugging on Gregory's sleeve as he clung to the ladder with his other hand. "I had a nightmare."

Sighing, Gregory rolled over to look at him full on. "And what do I have to do with that?" he asked, studying him.

The little boy blushed and ducked his head. "Can I sleep with you tonight? I promise I won't kick you!"

For a second, Gregory just stared at Jackson. "Um… okay," he finally mumbled, scooting over. Gregory never would have admitted it out loud, but he was glad for the company. Maybe it would keep his own nightmares at bay.

A smile broke across Jackson's face as he scrambled to lay down beside Gregory.

Having a sleeping mate wasn't new to Gregory. He and Grew used to share a room when they were little, but that had stopped when their father found out they shared a bed when they were scared.

But what five-year-old wouldn't have wanted a little comfort and security after a nightmare? And they found it from their twin brother. There was no way either of them would have gone to their parents, even their mother.

But when their father found out, he'd put a stop to it. He had thought it would make them weak and moved them to separate rooms almost instantly. That's when things had begun to change between them, and they began to compete against each other for their father's attention.

Deadlock

Sometime later, Gregory gripped the pillow tightly with both hands as he pressed his head hard against it. Gregory heard the sounds of Jackson moving around and yawning, and he knew it was time to get up.

So peeling himself away from the comfort of suffocating himself with his pillow, Gregory swung his legs over the edge of the bunk bed and jumped down and startled a 'yelp' out of the oldest Winfield child.

"How do you do that?" Jackson asked, his jaw hanging open as he stared at Gregory.

Gregory stood up and frowned at him. "How do I do what?" he asked as he brushed his hair back.

Jackson quickly scrambled down the ladder. "Jump down like that without hurting yourself."

Blinking, Gregory glanced up at the top bunk and frowned. He honestly hadn't thought it was all that high, so he just shrugged. "I don't know," he said. "Come on, get dressed or we're going to get into trouble." Not that Gregory actually thought the Winfields would do anything to either of them.

Not like his father would have if he'd been late for breakfast, but the threat was enough to get Jackson to drop the subject and hurry to get out of his PJs. Five minutes later, they were both dressed and hurrying down the stairs and into the kitchen.

Not surprisingly, Mrs. Winfield was already there and smiled when she saw them. "Good morning, boys," she said.

"Jackson, why don't you go grab your breakfast?"

The little boy nodded before scurrying into the kitchen. Gregory moved to follow, but Esther put her arm out and stopped him. Inwardly, he groaned, already knowing what was coming.

"Jonathan told me what happened last night," Esther said, sighing as she placed a hand on Gregory's cheek, and he forced himself not to flinch away. "I wish you could see that we care about you and want you to stay here with us."

"Like I told Mr. Winfield," Gregory said, stepping around her. "Talk to your friend before you say something like that." Not giving her a chance to respond, he hurried into the kitchen and went to help Jackson pour his cereal before he dumped it onto the ground.

Once Gregory was finished with helping Jackson, he poured himself another bowl (this was one of the few foods the Winfields ate that he'd had before) and they both went and sat down at the table.

"My friend Matthew was talking about this new TV show his family's watching, where these people travel through this wormhole and fight aliens," Jackson said, shoving his cereal into his mouth as he talked. "Have you ever seen it, Greggy? Mom and Dad won't let us watch anything like that."

"TV—" *Oh, right!* The entertainment box his dad had never allowed them to use. "Um…no. We didn't have a TV," Gregory said, eating his own cereal. "So I have no idea what you're talking about."

"Yeah…," Jackson said, pouting. "We aren't allowed to watch TV either. But *everyone* else we know does."

Esther sighed as she entered the kitchen. "Jackson, do you want to repeat to me what you were just saying?" she asked, placing her hands on her hips as she frowned down at him before giving him a small smile and kissing him on the forehead. "Just remember, Matthew's mother makes him eat vegetables with every meal."

For a second, Esther reminded Gregory so much of his mother, not that he remembered too much about her anymore.

Grimacing, Gregory set his spoon down and stood up, quickly depositing his dishes into the sink. He rested against the counter, taking in a deep breath and closing his eyes for a moment.

His mother was dead. She was gone, and had been gone for a long time now. So why was this bothering him so much? It took all his willpower to keep the moisture in his eyes from coming out.

Deadlocks don't cry.

"Gregory?" Esther said softly from behind him. "Are you alright?"

"What?" Gregory said, snapping out of his reverie as he spun around to face her. "Oh, yes, I'm fine." He cleared his throat and stood up straight, ignoring the urge to salute her. He was pretty sure that wouldn't help his situation.

"You're acting a bit off today," Esther said, frowning as she stepped forward. She reached out and placed the back of her hand against Gregory's forehead. "Well, you're not warm. You're sure you're feeling alright?" she asked, and Gregory squeezed his eyes shut.

He couldn't even remember when his father had asked him how he was. So why did this woman he barely knew care? "I... um... I didn't sleep so well last night," Gregory said, swallowing as he opened his eyes again. "But it wasn't a big deal."

"Good," Esther said, nodding as she studied Gregory. "Because Jonathan has plans for you today."

"Did I hear my name?" Jonathan asked, stepping into the kitchen. He ruffled up Jackson's hair as he turned toward Gregory and Esther. "What are you two talking about that involves me?"

"Oh... I was just telling Gregory I was glad he wasn't too tired for your plans," Esther said, grinning. "I'm sure he's just going to *love* them, even with this snow we got last night."

Gregory glanced out the window behind him and stopped when he realized how white it was outside. "Snow? Already?" he asked, frowning.

Jonathan laughed. "Yep, and from what I've heard, it's normal here," he said. "That's why I grabbed you this." He tossed Gregory a gray coat. "You're going to need it."

"Why?" Gregory asked, frowning as he pulled on the

coat and glanced around the kitchen. He *really* didn't like the way Esther was grinning or the smirk Jonathan had on his face. "What's going on?"

"We've a few things to deal with," Jonathan said, spinning his car keys around. "So let's get going."

Gregory grimaced. "I don't really like the sound of that."

Chuckling, Jonathan nodded his head toward the door. "Come on, let's get going, or we're going to be late," he said. "So get a move on it."

Sighing, Gregory nodded. "Right… but I have a feeling that I'm not going to like whatever we're going to do."

CHAPTER 21

It was a while later when Gregory glanced out the window and groaned. "This is my punishment, isn't it?"

Jonathan gave him a small smile and nodded as he pulled into the Church parking lot. "Yes, it is. You know, you're a pretty perceptive kid."

Gregory snorted. "Yeah, I kind of have to be," he mumbled under his breath as he ran his hand through his hair. "So… what exactly is my punishment? I assume it's not just going to church again."

"No, it's not," Jonathan said with a laugh. "Do you see the guy standing there by the door? That's Mr. Burton. He'll tell you what he wants you to do, and I want you to listen to him. Okay? He might be a little rough around the edges, but I want you to treat him with respect."

"Yes, sir," Gregory said, grabbing the car handle and shoving the door open. He was just climbing out when Jonathan said his name. "Yeah?" he asked, ducking his head back down to look at the man.

Deadlock

"Please, stay out of trouble," Jonathan said, gripping the steering wheel tightly as he pressed his lips together. "This is a punishment for what you did on Sunday, but I don't want you to make it worse."

Gregory nodded. "Yes, sir. I won't cause any trouble."

"Good. Oh, and… don't beat up any of the other boys," Jonathan said, grinning. "Alright? I *really* don't want to have to tell Esther. Even if your fight was for a good reason."

He nodded again. *Doesn't that fall under causing trouble?* he wondered but didn't say it out loud. If Mr. Winfield felt like he needed to say it again, he'd let him. "Understood, sir," he said, then with that, he closed the car door. He shoved his hands into his pockets as he started toward the church where the older man was waiting for him, skirting around the black sedan as he headed toward the door.

"Hello," Mr. Burton said, holding his hand out to him. "Gregory, right?"

"Yes, sir," he said, shaking the man's hand. "And you're Mr. Burton. I was told you would know what I'm here for."

Mr. Burton chuckled. "I suppose I do," he said. "Come on then, the other boys are already here."

Other boys? Great. This just got *so* much better.

Gregory kept his head up straight and his shoulders back as Mr. Burton led him around the side of the church to the wall where the boys had graffitied. There were already a few other boys scattered around the area, and Gregory guessed they were the vandals, though he didn't really remember what they looked like, nor did he really care.

They ignored Gregory and Mr. Burton as Mr. Burton led him to a couple of buckets sitting next to the wall. "Here's the paint you'll be using," he said, patting one of the buckets. "The brushes are over there, and I'll let you get started."

Grimacing, Gregory knelt next to one of the buckets and pulled on the lid, but it didn't come off easily, and he wasn't sure what to do. Painting wasn't exactly something his father had thought was important for him to learn to keep his cover. Looked like his father was wrong for once.

Shaking away that thought, Gregory rubbed his head and looked the bucket over. What was he missing? Gregory was still staring down at the paint can, trying to figure out how the heck you were supposed to open it when one of the boys walked up to him.

"So… do you have magical powers that you're trying to use to open that can?" the boy asked, tilting his head as he slouched against a dry part of the wall beside them. "Or should I do it?"

"Knock yourself out," Gregory said, shoving the can toward him as he stood up. "I don't care."

The boy smirked. "Knock myself out?" he repeated as he glanced around him. "I think I'll open the can instead." With that, he grabbed an oddly shaped screwdriver and shoved it against the lid.

Deadlock

The boy looked familiar, but Gregory couldn't place him. Maybe he'd been one of the boys he'd fought, but he was pretty sure he wasn't. Then again, it was all kind of a blur, so who knew? Maybe he had, maybe he hadn't.

"There," the boy said, finally popping the lid open and standing. "No magical powers required."

Gregory nodded and took the can. "Thanks."

"No problem. I'm Cody," he said, holding his hand out to Gregory. "I don't think we actually met last time I saw you. Though, the last time I saw you, you were in the middle of a foursome fight." Shrugging, he grinned at him. "So, that might have had something to do with it."

"Oh, right. I'm Gregory."

Cody nodded. "Cool name," he said, picking up the paintbrushes and tossing one to Gregory.

Gregory snorted as he spun it around. "I've always been partial to it."

Laughing, Cody nodded. "That's good to hear; I'm sure your parents are glad too."

"Yeah." *Though, I don't think they'd really ever cared.* "Um… How did you know how to open that thing?" Gregory asked, nodding to the paint can as he played with the brush in his hands. "It's worse than a Chinese puzzle box."

Cody glanced down at the bucket and shrugged. "Well, this isn't the first time I've had to do something like this."

Gregory just grunted. "Why am I not surprised?"

"I think I should take offense at that," Cody said, eyeing Gregory.

"Yeah," Gregory agreed, nodding. "But you're not going to, because you're not like those other boys." He nodded toward the other boys that were already painting at the other end of the church (as far from Gregory as they could). "Are you?"

"No, and I don't think you are either," Cody said, looking down inside the bucket and grinning. "Whoa, such a great color, don't you think?" he asked, tipping it to the side so Gregory could see it.

Gregory stepped forward and raised his eyebrow. "It's… green."

"What?!" Cody cried, looking back inside the can. "I thought it was gray." They were both silent. "Yeah… that was kind of lame wasn't it?"

Gregory glanced around and frowned. "Were you one of the boys who spray-painted the wall?" he asked. Though he was pretty sure he didn't fight this boy, that didn't mean he wasn't there. "Is that why you're here?"

"No, I didn't," Cody said, dipping his paintbrush and starting work. "But I didn't exactly try and stop them either."

Frowning, Gregory moved to dip his brush too, watching to see what he was supposed to do next. "And you're being punished because of that?" he asked as they both started to paint the side of the church.

Cody gave him a lopsided smile as he moved to catch some of the paint Gregory had dumped onto the wall. "Kind of," he said. "Why are you being punished? I *know* you didn't spray-paint this stuff."

Snorting, Gregory moved to get more paint. "I'm being punished because I punched a kid."

"Um... I think it was more than 'punched'," Cody said, glancing toward Gregory. "Don't you think?"

Before Gregory could respond, a commotion came from the other side of the parking lot. "Get out of my way, dweeb," one of the other boys growled, and both Gregory and Cody turned toward him.

"Oh, goody," Cody mumbled. "David's here."

"That the one I choked?" Gregory asked, glancing toward the boy again as they went back to their painting. The boy looked familiar, but that whole day was kind of a blur now, and Gregory wasn't really thinking about what he was doing at the time.

Cody nodded. "Yeah, he is, and trust me, he deserved it," he said. "I've thought about doing it myself a time or two, or twenty."

Gregory grimaced. "Yeah, but I almost killed him too," he said, and he didn't know why that thought was unsettling.

Snorting, Cody continued to paint. "I wouldn't have let

you go *that* far."

"Really?" Gregory said, glancing toward the other boy. "And you think you could have stopped me?"

"Oh, I know it," Cody said, smirking as he held up his paintbrush. "I could have easily taken you on."

"Sure…" Gregory said, smirking as he dipped his brush again. "Because it's not like I easily took the other three boys down."

Cody looked at him and grinned. "Exactly!"

CHAPTER 22

For a while, both Gregory and Cody fell into silence as they continued to paint the side of the Church, though Cody spent most of his time commenting about fixing the mess Gregory left when he put too much paint on the wall.

Gregory glanced away from the wall when Mr. Burton came out of the church. "Alright, boys, lunchtime!" he called, placing a tray of sandwiches down on the bed of one of the trucks parked nearby. "Don't want your parents thinking we're starving you."

Almost instantly, a wave of boys headed toward him, but both Gregory and Cody stayed where they were until the other boys had left again. Then they made their way over to the truck. Cody grabbed two sandwiches, tossing one to Gregory as he dropped onto the tailgate and began to unwrap another sandwich.

Hesitating, Gregory moved to lean against the truck but decided not to sit on it. He looked down at his sandwich and frowned. "Why are you hanging out with me?" he asked, glancing over at him. "I assume you at least know those other boys, so why aren't you over there with them? You don't even know me."

Cody glanced around and scooted a little closer to Gregory. "Alright, you caught me," he whispered. "I was secretly sent by the government to get close to you and find out if you're a psychopathic killer or not. Why else would I talk to you?" He rolled his eyes and turned back to his sandwich. "Those other boys aren't exactly friends."

"Well, I wouldn't 'exactly' know what a friend is," Gregory said, pulling off his coat and tying it around his waist. "What exactly do you use them for?"

Cody snorted and coughed. "I'm glad I haven't started to eat yet, or you would have made me choke with that," he said. "Do you seriously not know what a friend is 'for'?"

Before Gregory could think up a response, one of the other boys made their way over toward them. "Hey, you!" he spat, stabbing Gregory in the chest with his finger. "That was my shirt."

Glancing down, Gregory realized he was wearing one of the shirts Mrs. Winfield had given him. He supposed this boy's family must have given it to the Winfields, so looking up again, he smirked. "I thought it smelled funny when I put it on."

"What did you just say?" the boy said, grabbing Gregory by the front of his shirt.

Gregory fought the urge to punch the boy in the face

right then and there. The thing that stopped him was the fact that he didn't want to deal with the Winfields afterward.

Instead, he twisted his arm around and broke the boy's grip off of his shirt as he shoved him back with his other hand. Momentarily forgetting that his other hand was the one holding his uneaten sandwich.

At least if the Winfields asked, he'd say he'd forgotten.

His sandwich smashed into the front of the other boy's shirt, staining it with mayonnaise and mustard. "Oops," Gregory said, grimacing as he dropped the sandwich.

"That was your fault," the boy snapped, jabbing Gregory in the chest again. "And you did that on purpose, so apologize!"

"It wasn't my fault," Gregory said, gritting his teeth as he glared at the boy. "And I'm not going to apologize. *Especially* to someone like you." Apologizing was *not* something a Deadlock ever did.

"I said apologize," the boy growled, stepping closer to Gregory as if he thought he could actually intimidate him into doing it.

Gregory laughed. "Make me."

"Oh, really?!"

It was at that moment Cody jumped down from the truck bed and stepped between Gregory and the other boy, and he didn't seem at all daunted by the fact that the other boy was much taller than him (not that it had daunted

Gregory either).

"Hey, Michael," Cody said, holding up his hands and keeping the older boy back. "How about instead, you go snort paint fumes somewhere else, like that *other* stuff you like to snort? Catch my drift?"

"Are you threatening me?" Michael asked, glaring at Cody.

Cody gave him a small smile. "Of course!" he said. "Would you listen to anything less?"

Michael glared at him. "Just tell *him*." He nodded toward Gregory with a glare. "To stay out of my way."

"I'm sure he will," Cody said, then with a low growl, Michael spun around and marched away, and Cody dropped his hands down to his side.

"How'd you know that would work?" Gregory asked, huffing as he crossed his arms and turned toward Cody.

"His pupils were dilated and he had stuff around his nose," Cody said, shrugging as he turned back to the bed of the truck. "Besides, I've had a feeling for a while. I'm sure it's going to catch up to him soon."

Gregory grabbed up another sandwich, and this time, he hopped up onto the back of the truck next to Cody. "You know, I could have taken him on," he said. "He was all bark and no bite."

"Yeah, and if you'd taken him on you wouldn't have gotten into trouble?" Cody asked with a laugh before he closed his eyes and bowed his head.

Deadlock

It took Gregory a second to realize that he was... *What did they call it again? Praying!* That's what he was doing. Gregory waited until the boy opened his eyes again before clearing his throat.

Cody glanced over at him and frowned. "What?"

"Oh, nothing!" Gregory said, glancing down at his sandwich as he bit his lip. "It's just... you... *pray* too?"

"Yeah," Cody said, turning toward him as he brought his feet up onto the bed of the truck. He looked at Gregory's face and laughed. "It does seem a little weird, doesn't it? I remember thinking the same thing."

"No kidding!" Gregory said, rolling his eyes. "I don't get it. Why do you have to do it? So you don't choke on your food?"

"I didn't grow up in a Christian home either, so I get it," Cody said, shrugging as he bit into his sandwich. "I used to think it was strange too, but no, it's not so you don't choke on your food."

"Strange?" Gregory said as he started to eat. "I suppose that's *one* word for it, though it's not exactly the word I would have used."

Cody cleared his throat and twisted the sandwich around in his hands. "Look," he finally said. "I'm still kind of new at this *stuff* myself, but if you... you know, have any questions, I'll try to answer them."

Gregory sighed. "Depending on what happens, I might take you up on that."

"Good," Cody said, finishing off his sandwich and shoving the wrapper into his pocket. "Well, once you're done, we'd better get back to painting." With a nod, Gregory finished his sandwich, and they went back to work.

It was getting late, and the sun was already setting by the time they were almost finished with the wall. It wasn't as if they could do too much painting in the dark anyway, so when some of the boys' parents showed up, they started to clean up.

"See you around, Gregory," Cody said, grabbing a backpack sitting next to the wall. "Though, I think this is the only day we have to do this. So… It might be a while."

Gregory nodded as he pulled his coat back on. "You have someone coming to pick you up?" he asked.

"Nah… I'm just going to walk. You?" Cody asked.

"No!" Gregory snorted. "The Winfields live too far out of town for that, especially in this weather."

Cody smirked. "Big baby. Can't handle hiking through a little snow?"

"Big baby?" Gregory repeated. "You know, Cody, you really shouldn't talk to yourself like that."

"Ah… you're as funny as an angry cat," Cody said as they both headed toward the end of the parking lot.

"Yeah," Gregory said, shaking his head. "Because *that* makes sense?"

"It did in my head, and that's all that matters," Cody said, shrugging as they stopped at the entrance to the

Deadlock

Church.

"Sounds like your head's a scary place," Gregory said, just as he spotted the Winfields' car headed toward them. "Looks like my ride's actually here."

Cody nodded. "That's my cue to get going myself," he said, pulling up his hood. "See you around, Gregory."

CHAPTER 23

Gregory grabbed the car door and scrambled inside the Winfields' car, buckling up and slouching back against the seat as he watched Cody head in the other direction. He shook himself when Mr. Winfield cleared his throat.

"How'd it go?" Jonathan asked, glancing over at Gregory as he pulled back out of the church parking lot.

"I know you probably don't want me to say this," Gregory said, shrugging. "But it actually wasn't that bad." He'd had much worse punishments. "I mean… it's not my favorite pastime, but still."

"Huh." Jonathan frowned. "Really?"

Gregory nodded. "Yeah. I don't know a lot about painting, but I think I did alright, though I'm not volunteering for *more* work, just so you know." Jonathan chuckled at that, then they both fell silent for the rest of the drive back to the Winfields' house.

They were just pulling up when something caught Gregory's eye. It was the black sedan that had been parked outside of the church earlier when Jonathan had dropped him off. Raising an eyebrow, he glanced over at Jonathan.

"I can see you've got 'company'," Gregory said, grimacing.

"Yeah, Esther called me about that," Jonathan said, clearing his throat as he pulled the car to a stop. "Um… Agent White's dropping by, you know, um, he asked if he could after we told him the word you gave us."

Gregory froze, then slowly nodded. "And that just slipped your mind? Did it?" he asked. "And what I gave you wasn't a word; it was a name." With a long sigh, he shoved his door open and climbed out.

He might as well get this over with.

Jonathan climbed out a second later, and they both headed toward the front door, where they found Mrs. Winfield waiting for them. "Oh, Gregory!" she said, grabbing his arm. "I'm so glad you're back. Ben's here, and he brought a friend here to see you."

"Yeah, Mr. Winfield just mentioned that," Gregory said. "Though…" He frowned and glanced over at Jonathan. "He didn't mention anyone else being here."

Esther gave him a small smile. "Well, I'm sorry about that," she said. "Anyway, the children are upstairs, so why don't you come help me in the kitchen?" she asked Jonathan as she switched from grabbing on to Gregory's arm to Jonathan's, before tugging him down the hall. "They're waiting for you in the living room, Gregory."

Before he could respond, they were both gone.

Gregory bit his lip as he glanced toward the living room, then slipping off his shoes, he quietly crept forward until he had his back pressed up against the wall just outside of the living room.

"Now, you're sure he said 'Deadlock'?" he heard a stranger's voice say. "A hundred percent sure?"

Gregory peeked around the corner and into the living room, quickly taking in the scene of the two men talking. One he knew as Agent White, but the other man looked slightly familiar too. It took him a second before he realized where he'd seen the man before, and the black sedan clicked in his head.

The man was the stranger Gregory had seen talking to the boy outside the church, the one who'd seemed familiar even then. *Who are you?* Gregory wondered.

"For the hundredth time, yes," Agent White said, rubbing the bridge of his nose as he paced the living room.

"Are you sure?" the man asked again as he shoved himself away from the wall and took a step toward Agent White. "Because…"

"It was Deadlock," Gregory said, stepping into the living room as he crossed his arms. "And I'm a hundred percent sure of that."

The man spun around to face him. "Blimey," he whispered, staring at Gregory as he took a step back from him. "He looks just like her, Ben! He really *was* telling the truth, and you were right."

Gregory wasn't sure what the man meant, but he didn't like it. "I know who he is," he said, with a nod toward Agent White. "But who are you?"

The man shot a glance toward Agent White but kept his gaze on Gregory as if trying to decide what to say. For a moment they both seemed to be sizing each other up, then Agent White broke the silence.

"Gregory, this is the friend I told you at church I was meeting," he said, placing a hand on the man's shoulder. "Special Agent Justin Huntley, meet Gregory... I suppose it's Deadlock, isn't it?"

The man hesitated a second before adding, "Janet Huntley is my sister."

Gregory blinked and it took a second for the name to register, and when it did his jaw dropped. "My mom?"

"Yes, Gregory," Agent Huntley said, giving him a small smile. "I'm your uncle."

"No," Gregory said, shaking his head as he took a step back from him. "My mother didn't have any family, she would have told us if she had a... a brother!"

Agent Huntley snorted. "When going undercover, you don't exactly tell the criminals who they should go after if they find out who you really are," he said. "That wouldn't exactly be the best move."

Gregory's head was spinning. It couldn't be true! *Undercover?* His mother was... a mole? But that didn't make any sense!

"Why should I believe you?" Gregory asked, his gaze snapping back to where Agent Huntley was standing. "For all I know, you're lying about *all* of this."

Agent Huntley cleared his throat. "When I was told someone had contacted Ben about Deadlock, I… I went and got this," he said. "I… I was hoping that… that whoever it was would know Jan, at least in passing. I wasn't expecting you." He hesitated a second before holding a photo out to Gregory. "Here."

Frowning, Gregory took one step forward and took it from him. It was a picture of his mother alright, but way younger than he'd ever seen, and she was… standing next to a younger version of the man standing in front of him now.

"Where is she?" Agent Huntley asked. "I mean, did she leave Deadlock too?"

Gregory winced. "When… when was the last time you heard from her?" he asked, looking up at the agent as he held the picture tightly in his hand.

Agent Huntley sighed and dropped his gaze to his hands as he rubbed them against each other. "We lost contact with her," he whispered. "Shortly after she found out she was pregnant with… I guess you."

Grimacing, Gregory sighed, "So you don't know."

Huntley's gaze shot up, and he locked eyes with Gregory. "Don't know what?" he asked.

Deadlock

"She's… dead," Gregory said.

Pain flickered across the agent's face before he gained control of himself again. "When?"

Gregory shifted uncomfortably. "Almost five years ago."

"Five years?" Agent Huntley whispered, staring off into space as he dropped himself down onto the couch. "I wasn't even there for her." He groaned and buried his face in his hands as he rested his elbows on his knees.

Gregory wasn't sure why, but this stranger's reaction to his mother's death made him mad.

"I wasn't there either," Gregory said, taking a step toward Agent Huntley, ignoring the other agent now standing behind him. "And now you're telling me she was a mole? What for? Why… Oh, my word! She was there for Father, wasn't she? She was undercover to bring Deadlock down!"

That realization caused Gregory's mind to spiral out of control completely.

He knew. His father knew about his mother being a spy. *He wouldn't have… he wouldn't have killed her!* Oh, how Gregory wished he could believe that, but he couldn't. He knew his father too well for that.

With a sudden lurch, Gregory dropped to his knees just feet from his mother's brother. He couldn't help it, he started to cry. Cry like he'd wanted to when he'd first learned his mother was dead.

But now his father wasn't there to stop him. Now

Gregory knew why he wanted to stop him. And it hurt, it all hurt, like nothing he'd ever felt before. Not when even when Roman had put him through the most grueling training.

So Gregory just cried.

CHAPTER 24

Agent Justin Huntley didn't seem to know what to do, which Gregory was grateful for. The last thing he wanted was for this man to try and comfort him when all he wanted to do was cry out the tears he'd been holding back for years.

Finally, the tears began to slow and Gregory started to feel embarrassed as he scrambled to his feet. "I'm sorry," he said, wiping his face and fighting to gain control of himself again. "I shouldn't be crying like a baby."

"How old are you, Gregory?" Agent Huntley asked, shoving himself out of the couch and taking a step toward him.

Gregory sniffed and quickly wiped his nose. "I'll be thirteen in a few months," he said. "Why do you ask?"

Huntley sighed. "Because you're just a kid, and I have a feeling you have a *lot* to cry about," he said. "You shouldn't be sorry about it."

"How much do you know about Deadlock?" Gregory growled. "Because if you believe that, it's obviously not very much." He stepped toward the agent… his 'uncle' and glared at him. "Don't act like you know *everything* about me."

"In that case… Are you ready to talk?" Agent White asked, placing a hand on Gregory's shoulder. "Because we're ready when you are. Personally, I'd like to know what the son of DL is doing here."

"Yeah," Gregory whispered, nodding as he took in a deep breath. "I'm ready to get my 'story' over with, but I'd like the Winfields to be in here for this, so I don't have to repeat it again for them."

"I'll go get them," Agent White offered, giving Gregory a slight smile before he let go of his shoulder and hurried out of the living room to find the Winfields. Gregory let out a long breath before he moved and leaned back against the wall, crossing his arms.

He could do this! But Gregory wasn't sure he wanted to. Once he said it he couldn't take it back. Things with the Winfields would never be the same, even if he did keep *some* of his secrets.

Sighing, he closed his eyes, and for a second, he thought about praying to their God, but quickly shook that thought away. A moment later, Jonathan and Esther stepped into the room, followed closely by Agent White.

Wordlessly, they all sat down. Gregory looked around him at the four people looking at him and realized he didn't know where to start! As it turned out, he wasn't the only one who felt awkward.

Deadlock

"How about something to eat?" Mrs. Winfield asked, jumping to her feet.

"Honey," Jonathan said, gently taking her arm and pulling her back down. "I think Gregory probably just wants to get this over with."

"Yes, of course!" she said, clasping her hands together as she reluctantly sat back down.

Gregory took in a deep breath. "I... I don't... I don't really know where I should start," he whispered. "I guess with Deadlock." He cleared his throat. "Deadlock is... well, they're... we are...the thing is..."

"Deadlock is a terrorist group," Agent Huntley said, glancing at Gregory before he continued. "Not a lot is currently known about them, except for the fact that they are linked with major events all the way back to the 1600s, maybe even further back than that. Other than that, not much is actually known about them. Gregory?"

Though he was glad he didn't have to explain that part (since he really couldn't), Gregory still wasn't sure if he was ready to tell them the truth about why he was there. How would they respond to the fact that he was supposed to kill Jonathan?

"My family..." Gregory grimaced. "My family founded Deadlock. My name is Gregory Deadlock, and my father currently runs the... organization. A few weeks ago I left, and that's how I ended up here with you guys."

"There's something I don't understand... Deadlock

doesn't just let people leave," Huntley said, crossing his arms as he studied Gregory for a second. "Especially a member of the founding family."

"I… I wasn't planning on leaving," Gregory whispered, running his hand through his hair. "It was part of my test."

"And what was your test?" Agent White asked, frowning.

Glancing toward the Winfields, who had stayed silent so far, Gregory grimaced and looked down. "I'd rather not say."

Huntley sighed before moving forward and squatted down in front of him. "It's alright, Gregory," he said, reaching up and placing his hand on Gregory's arm. "We're here to help you. I *want* to help you."

"You answer me a question first," Gregory said, looking down at him as he narrowed his eyes. "What were you doing at the church earlier today? And don't pretend you weren't; I saw your black sedan."

Chuckling, Agent Huntley stood up. "You're observant, I'm glad," he said, glancing toward Agent White. "I wasn't there because of you if that's what you're thinking. Honestly, I wasn't sure if you were going to be there or not; I just had a feeling you might be."

Gregory narrowed his eyes. "So what? You were watching me?" he asked, then he shook himself. "Wait, no, because you didn't know what I looked like until I stepped into this room. So what were you doing?"

"I can't tell you that," Agent Huntley said, shaking his head. "I'm sorry, Gregory. It's classified."

Deadlock

Snorting, Gregory crossed his arms. "And you don't think what you want me to tell you about Deadlock, we consider classified?"

The two agents exchanged a glance. "We?" Agent White asked. "You still consider yourself a part of Deadlock? Is that why you won't tell us what your little test was about?"

"What?!" Gregory said, shaking his head. "No, that... that's not why." *Not that the real reason is much better.* "Even if it *was*, it's really none of your business."

"Gregory, what was your test?" Mr. Winfield asked, stepping in between them. "Just tell us, and get the secrets out of the way."

Get the secrets out of the way? Gregory was afraid that would be something that could never happen. "I was sent to watch you," he whispered, looking toward Jonathan as he swallowed. "He called you the 'Preacher'. I guess I understand why now because you are a preacher. Though, I didn't know it at the time."

"Why me?" Jonathan asked as Esther stood up and moved to stand behind him, and he seemed to instinctively wrap his arm around her.

"I don't know," Gregory said, the lie easy enough to say, even if he hadn't been trained all his life to lie. "Father... he... All he said was you were causing trouble, and I needed to keep an eye on you."

The color drained from Esther's face. "Why?" she asked. "What have we done that would cause... these people to pay attention to us?"

"I… think I can answer that." Gregory cleared his throat as he crossed his arms and dropped his gaze to the ground. "De los Muertos has… close connections with my family and Deadlock," he said, grimacing. "If I had to guess, I'd say Father didn't like you getting involved. It's not good for business."

Chuckling, Agent White glanced toward Mr. Winfield and shrugged. "I guess we were right," he said. "You were making a difference there after all." Before any of them could say anything, there was a buzzing sound.

"Sorry," Agent Huntley said, reaching into his pocket and pulling something out. "I need to take this." Everyone turned toward him as he held a mobile phone to his ear and headed out of the room.

The second they were looking away and not paying attention to him anymore, Gregory slipped out of the living room and through the window. No one even noticed him as he opened the window and climbed out of it.

He was running across the yard before any of them could come after him. He didn't stop until he was deep into the woods that surrounded the Winfields' house, and the building became an object among the trees.

It was at that moment realization of what he'd just done came crashing down on him, and his knees buckled.

"What are you doing, Gregory?!" he yelled, burying his face in his hands as his heart thudded against his chest, and he found it harder and harder to breathe with every second that passed.

Gregory knew he could never go back now. There was no coming back from a betrayal like this. Were the Winfields really worth it? He didn't know! He just wanted to be normal, but could he ever be?

Pivoting around, and back to his feet, Gregory smacked his fist against the trunk of the nearest tree and was grateful for the blood that dripped down his knuckles a second later. It was the only pain he seemed to be able to control.

It was then that Gregory realized he'd already made his choice. He'd chosen this family he barely knew (but wanted to be a part of) over everything he'd ever known. What had he done?

CHAPTER 25

Once he had himself under control again, Gregory slipped back into the house, then to the bathroom where he cleaned his hand the best he could. He was just wiping the last of the blood and water off his hands when he heard the bathroom door groan.

Gregory tensed for a second before the person knocked on the door. "Gregory?" Agent Huntley called it. "Are you in there?"

"Yes," Gregory sighed, opening the door. "Was there something you needed?" he asked, crossing his arms as he leaned against the door, making sure to keep his one hand tucked under his arm.

"I just… came to say goodbye," Huntley said, clearing his throat as he tugged at the collar of his shirt. "And… make you sure you were doing alright with all of this."

"Why do you care?" Gregory asked, squinting at him. "Do you think being nice to me is going to make me want to tell you everything that I know about Deadlock? Because that's not going to work."

"I know that this might be hard for you to understand, considering how you no doubt grew up," Hunter said, sighing. "But I do care. I cared a great deal about my sister, and you're the only connection I have to her now."

Gregory glared at him. "I'm not my mother, so don't expect me to be like her."

Agent Huntley gave him a small smile. "I know Deadlock better than most," he said, his eyes burning into Gregory. "I know they didn't send you to just *watch* Pastor Jonathan. But I can understand why you wouldn't want to tell them that part."

"Are… are you going to tell them?" Gregory whispered.

"No, because I can't help thinking the part of you that stopped you was also the part of you that came from my sister," he said, then he reached out his hand and placed it on Gregory's shoulder. "I think you're a good person, Gregory, and if you need help… I don't want you to hesitate to call me."

With that, Agent Huntley tucked a card into his pocket, turned, and headed out of the Winfields' house.

Once he was gone, Gregory shook himself and quickly hurried down the hallway to Jackson's bedroom. He hurried inside, checked to make sure Jackson wasn't there, then he closed and locked the door.

Was he like his mother? he wondered as he started to pace. He didn't really remember her, yet he wanted it to be true. But how could it be? Especially if she was really a mole inside Deadlock the whole time.

Had she even loved Grew and himself? Gregory quickly shoved that thought away. "It doesn't matter; she's gone," he whispered, flopping down into a pile of Jackson's stuffed toys and groaning.

Later that day, Gregory was glad when Mr. and Mrs. Winfield didn't press him for more information about Deadlock during dinner. Even though it did turn out to be a very awkward dinner.

Thankfully, the awkwardness seemed to slowly disperse over the next twenty-four-hours. And for a short time, Gregory thought things could go back to the way they had been.

As it was, the next day, Gregory found himself clearing the table off after Mia, and Jackson found reasons to get out of it. Oddly enough, he didn't mind. Cleaning up after himself was something he'd always done.

There was something so *normal* about having to clean the dishes himself, instead of just piling his metal dishes up on top of everyone else's. So that's where Mrs. Winfield found him when she came back in with the mail, trying to clean the dishes, but not doing a very good job of it.

"Gregory, you got something," Mrs. Winfield said as she flipped through the mail.

Gregory froze and slowly lowered the bowl he was trying to figure out how to clean. "I did?" he whispered, wiping the soap and water off his hands as he stepped toward her. Other than the FBI agents, the Winfields were the only ones who knew he was there. Weren't they?

"Here," Mrs. Winfield said, and Gregory's heart started to thud against his chest as she absentmindedly held a white envelope out to him.

Reluctantly taking it, Gregory moved back to the table and sat down. He placed it on the palm of his right hand and moved it up and down, frowning. It was too light to be an explosive, and too heavy to be a deadly poison of some kind. So what was it?

The odd lump at the center told him that *something* was inside it, and not just a letter.

That fact alone made it where he wasn't sure he wanted to open it. But what choice did he have? The last thing he needed was someone *else* opening it for him.

So biting his bottom lip, Gregory grabbed a butter knife still sitting on the table and quickly slit it open before he could change his mind. Carefully, he poured the contents of the envelope onto the table in front of him.

The second he saw the light glitter on the silver, he knew what they were, and his heart skipped a beat. Slowly, he reached out and ran his finger over the cold metal before snatching them up and tightening his grip around them until the metal bit into his skin.

They were Deadlock cufflinks, and even an idiot would know what they meant by sending them there for him.

Deadlock knew he was there. But did that mean they knew what he'd done, or at the very least, what he was planning on doing? He hadn't told the Winfields, but the longer he stayed with them, the easier he knew it would be to tell the FBI agents everything they wanted to know about DL.

If they knew… what was he going to do?! He was as good as dead; he knew that. They wouldn't let him talk if they could help it, and it wouldn't matter if he was their leader's son or not.

Gregory was thankful that Mrs. Winfield had already left the room as he rested his elbows on the table and buried his face in his hands. He wanted to scream but knew that wouldn't actually do him any good.

The truth was, he needed to talk to someone. But who? He couldn't tell the Winfields, and before now, he'd always gone to Grew. Though they'd fought, they'd always had each other's back, but he was obviously out of the question for this one.

So, besides the FBI agents, who else was there? Maybe… maybe he could explain it to Cody.

Sure, it might be hard to tell him everything, but the boy seemed reasonable enough, and he might actually listen to the whole thing before deciding anything. The problem was, he had no idea where to find him. But maybe there was a way he could…

Scrambling to his feet, Gregory pocketed the cufflinks

and hurried out of the dining room to find Jonathan. As it turned out, it didn't take him long.

He found him in one of the rooms on the far side of the house. Jackson told him it was his 'study', though in some ways it reminded Gregory of his dad's office, but in other ways it was very different.

The door was open, but Gregory hesitated to enter. If he'd ever entered his dad's office without permission, he would have been given extra 'training'. After a couple of seconds of debating with himself, Gregory knocked on the door and cleared his throat.

"Gregory," Jonathan said, looking up and smiling from where he sat behind the desk. "Come in."

"Sorry to bother you, sir," Gregory said, swallowing as he entered the study/office and clasped his hands behind his back. He really wasn't sure where to go from here. "Um… I was wanting to ask Mr. Burton about one of the other boys I painted the church with, and I was wondering if you knew where I could find him."

Jonathan leaned back and slowly nodded. "I was going to head out and help at the homeless shelter today," he said. "If you want to tag along, we can stop by the church first, and you can talk to Mr. Burton."

Biting his lip, Gregory glanced around as he shoved his hand into the pocket with the cufflinks, then he nodded. "Okay, that works," he said, nodding. "When are you planning on leaving?"

"Oh..." Mr. Winfield glanced at his watch. "How does half an hour sound?"

Gregory nodded. "Sounds fine, sir," he said, stepping back. "I'll just... go get ready to go." With that, he ducked out as fast as he could. He knew that Mr. Winfield wasn't his father, but it had always been a bad thing if his father had him come to his office, and those feelings had risen without warning.

Leaning against the wall outside in the hallway, Gregory quickly steadied his breath and shook himself.

If just the thought of his father's office did this to him, what would he do if he was forced to face him again? Grimacing, Gregory shoved himself away from the wall and hurried toward the stairs.

Hopefully, if that day ever came, it would be many years in the future.

CHAPTER 26

"Mr. Burton?" Gregory said, shoving his hands into his pockets as he glanced around the room Mr. Winfield had sent him to that was in the back of the church. It was packed with books and chairs. "Are you in here?"

"Yes, yes!" Mr. Burton said, his head appearing above one of the stacks of books. He looked at Gregory and frowned. "Oh, hello. Gregory, right?"

"Yes, sir," Gregory said, taking a cautious step forward.

"And what can I do for you, young man?" Mr. Burton asked, brushing his hair out of his face as he stood up and studied Gregory.

Gregory for his part quickly dropped his gaze to the ground. "Well, um… I was just…" He cleared his throat. "I was just wondering if you knew where I could find Cody, the boy I was painting with?"

"I'm sorry, I don't," Mr. Burton said, shaking his head as he moved around toward Gregory. "I'm not even quite sure who he is. He just showed up at the breakfast we offered the boys. I'm sorry, I wish I could be more help."

"It's fine," Gregory said, sighing as his shoulders drooped. "I knew it was a long shot, but thanks anyway." With that, Gregory quickly headed out of the church and to where Jonathan was waiting inside his car.

"Any luck?" Mr. Winfield asked, glancing over at Gregory as he slid into the passenger side and buckled up.

"No," Gregory said, shaking his head as he flopped his head back against the seat. "He doesn't even know who he is."

"I'm sorry," Jonathan said as he started up the car. "Well... I guess we'll head to the homeless shelter then. Though I'll try to keep an ear out to see if anyone else might know who he is."

Gregory shrugged. "Whatever, it doesn't matter. I was just curious." It was stupid for him to hope that Cody would understand about Deadlock anyway. If he'd said anything to him, he probably would have regretted it anyway.

It didn't take Jonathan long to pull to a stop behind an old brick building that Gregory assumed was the 'homeless shelter' Mr. Winfield had mentioned earlier.

Running his hand through his hair, Gregory climbed out and glanced around. "So... what do you... do here?" he asked.

"Well, we're here to help feed them today," Mr. Winfield said as he got out and made his way to Gregory's side of the car. "Come on." He nodded to the paint peeling door at the

Deadlock

back of the building. "I'll introduce you to everyone."

Oh, joy, Gregory thought, rolling his eyes the second Jonathan had his back to him. He was sure he was just going to *love* this. Straightening his shoulders, Gregory steeled himself for the torture to come.

He was pretty sure it wouldn't be like anything his father or Roman would have put him through. Though, he wasn't a hundred percent sure this would actually be much better than that.

In less than five minutes, Gregory had been introduced to several people; he had no intention of remembering their names for more than another ten to twenty minutes, maybe less.

"Is the food supposed to smell funny?" Gregory said, scrunching up his nose as he followed Mr. Winfield into the large kitchen in the back of the building. He honestly had no idea if it was supposed to or not.

Jonathan glanced over at him and laughed. "I don't think we have many complaints," he said. "Well... maybe a few. But it really doesn't smell *that* bad, just... strange. Like cafeteria food."

Gregory stopped walking, turned toward him, and frowned. "So... it *is* supposed to smell like that?"

After that they stood behind the counter, serving the food up to the people who came through. But this was *not* something Gregory cared to waste his day doing. It wasn't as if these people couldn't find jobs somewhere; his dad had hired homeless people like them all the time.

So once he started to run low on the food inside the dish he was serving, Gregory started to plot his escape. Ten minutes later, Gregory glanced toward Jonathan, who was chatting with the people at the end of the line, before taking his empty tray and heading to where they had more food.

Then, once he was sure no one was watching, Gregory slipped out the back door and into the alleyway behind the building. Hunching his shoulders against the cold wind blowing through the buildings, Gregory pulled up his hood and just started walking.

After avoiding the fifth pile of shattered glass, trash, and beer cans, it became obvious to Gregory what part of town the homeless shelter was set up in. The Winfields might live in a small town, but that didn't mean there wasn't a 'bad' part of town, and that was exactly where he was.

Not that Gregory was bothered by it; he was pretty sure he could take care of himself.

He heard talking and laughing not far from him. Gregory gradually slowed his pace to a crawl more than anything else.

Then making sure his hood covered his face, Gregory shoved his hands into his pockets and started forward again, already knowing what awaited him around the next corner.

In truth, hiring just any homeless person wasn't all that

Deadlock

common for Deadlock. No, homeless people who hung out in these kinds of places had always been more of their style. Those hiding from something, desperate for money, with nothing to lose.

Gregory hoped Jonathan stayed away from those kinds; they weren't safe to be around, unless you knew how to handle them.

"Hey!" Gregory heard someone yell as he turned the corner and kept walking. The next second, he felt a hand on his arm, and he reacted instinctively. He moved to the side, grabbed the person's wrist, pulled it off of him, and twisted their arm around, forcing them to their knees at an odd angle.

"That was a very stupid thing to do," Gregory hissed into the young man's ear. "Now, do you want me to break your arm, or something else?"

"How about instead, you just let him go?" someone behind Gregory said.

Turning, Gregory found the last person he expected standing there. "Cody?" he said, letting go of the young man's arm as he took a step back and continued to stare at the other kid. "What are you doing here?"

"Gregory?!" Cody said, his eyes growing wider for a split second, and he looked as surprised to see him there as Gregory was. "What are *you* doing here?"

Before he could respond, the young man who Gregory had shoved to the ground cut in. "Do you know this boy?"

he asked Cody.

Cody stood there, studying Gregory as he smoked something that Gregory was pretty sure wasn't a cigarette. "Barely," he said, blowing out a breath of smoke toward Gregory, who quickly covered his face with his arm. "What are you doing here, Gregory?"

"What are *you* doing here?" Gregory growled out, dropping his arm and stepping toward the other boy.

Gregory was starting to understand that his family weren't the best people in the world, but smoking was one thing his father had always said was something he and Grew were never to touch.

Ironic, really.

"Are you… *smoking?*" Gregory asked, sneering at the item in Cody's hand. "Don't you know how stupid that is?"

Cody snorted as he lowered the item from his mouth and sneered at Gregory. "And you would know about stupid, wouldn't you?"

"What did you just say?" Gregory said, stepping closer to him. "Say it again."

Laughing, Cody glanced toward the young man and then back at Gregory. "Why? I think you heard me, or are you deaf as well as stupid?" With that, Cody shoved Gregory hard in the chest. "Get out of my face!" he hissed. "Or you'll see if I can take you on like I said I could."

"Please," Gregory sneered, standing his ground. "I could take you down without even trying."

Deadlock

"Oh, yeah, right!" Cody scoffed. "You are so full of yourself."

Gregory narrowed his eyes and gripped his hands into fists. "Oh, really? Do you want to try me?"

"Maybe I do!" Cody growled back.

For a split second, Gregory thought about taking the boy down, but then he thought better of it. He didn't need to get himself or the Winfields into more trouble. "You know what? I don't care," Gregory said, holding up his hands and taking a step back. "It's your life. Ruin it if you want to by smoking that *stuff*, I really don't care."

"Thanks for your permission," Cody scoffed.

"You're welcome!" Gregory yelled, then with one final glare, he spun around and marched away.

CHAPTER 27

Gregory went several blocks before he stopped. Then, with a yell, he kicked the wall beside him. What had he been thinking? Of course he couldn't trust Cody; he should have known that!

Stupid, stupid stupid! he repeated in his head as he kicked the wall over and over again.

His eyes were burning, and he didn't know why. Finally, Gregory stopped kicking the wall and rested his forehead against the brick wall. What was wrong with him? Why was Cody acting this way? And why was it affecting him like this?

"Hey, kid," someone said behind him as he heard footsteps moving closer.

With a flash of anger, Gregory spun around toward them. "What do you want?!" he snapped. The next second, he felt a fist in his face. Gregory stumbled back, more out of surprise than the actual force of the punch.

When he turned toward the man again, he realized he

wasn't alone.

"What do you think you're doing?!" Gregory hissed, glaring the two men down. He quickly recognized them as two of his father's goons.

The one on the left laughed as he shook his hand out. "I think I'm punching you in the face."

"Do you know who I am?" Gregory growled, spitting blood out of his mouth as he glared at his father's goons and took a step toward them. "I asked you a question!" His anger mixed with the authority he'd always held with his father's men.

"We know exactly who you are," the goon on the right said, crossing his arms. "Why do you think we're here?"

Remembering their names, Gregory stared at Van and Gib. "He... he sent you for me?" Gregory whispered.

"Him... Roman... does it matter which?" Gib asked, shrugging. "The only thing that matters is... what the heck you think you're doing?!" With that, he stepped forward and slammed Gregory into the wall behind him. "Are you really so stupid that you're getting attached to your target?!"

"Finish the job," Van said, moving to Gregory's other side as he rested his hand on the gun in his waistband. "Or we'll finish you."

"What if I don't want to?" Gregory asked, glancing between the two of them as he shoved Gib's hand off his chest and stepped away from the wall. "Here's a crazy thought... What if I want out?"

Van and Gib looked at each other, then they both started laughing. "Gregory, you big idiot, that would be a crazy thought," Van said, shaking his head. "Because there is no getting out, especially for you."

"Really?" Gregory said, glaring up at him.

"Yes, really. You can even run, but we'll just keep coming for you, Gregory," Van hissed. "And we're not the only ones Roman sent."

Gregory squared his shoulders and nodded. "Thanks for the warning. But I want out, and I will get out!"

"Oh! Did you hear him, Van? He wants out," Gib scoffed, smirking down at Gregory. "Well, why didn't you just say so?! That changes everything. We'll just let you go, and we'll go back and tell Roman." He snorted. "Do you really think we're that stupid, Gregory? You're coming with us, and we're taking you home."

"Then someone else will be sent to finish your job," Van said, reaching for Gregory's arm, and that's when he acted on instinct.

He twisted around and kicked out at Gib, slamming his knee into his chest. Then he pivoted around and ducked under Van's arm.

With that, Gregory took off down the street, his boots thudding against the snow covered concrete as he ran as fast as his legs could carry him, knowing that Van and Gib wouldn't be able to keep up with him even if they tried.

Both his heart and his head were pounding by the time

Deadlock

he came to a stop sometime later. Gregory bent over, clutching his knees as he gulped in the cold air and tried to get himself to think straight.

What was he going to do? Deep down, Gregory knew that he wouldn't let Deadlock kill Jonathan. But what *could* he do? The people who would come for both him and the Winfields would be as well trained as he was, if not better.

He had to come up with a plan, but this wasn't something he'd been prepared for. What was he thinking? He was seriously going to turn against Deadlock for these people? His whole world? Everything and everyone he knew?

"Gregory, what are you doing?" he mumbled to himself as he ran his hand through his hair and stood up. His head was spinning, and he felt slightly sick. In truth, Gregory knew exactly what he was doing, and why.

The Winfields barely knew him, and most of what they thought they knew wasn't the truth. Yet, somehow, they still cared about him, more than his father ever had. So he'd protect them if he could from the danger they didn't even know was coming for them.

Fighting was one thing he was good at.

Though for now, all he could do was hope that Van and Gib would stay in town, at least until Gregory could figure out what to do. Of course… that didn't mean that someone else wouldn't come, and he needed to get ready for it.

When Gregory finally looked around him, he realized

he wasn't far from the Winfields' house.

Huh. Hopefully, Mr. Winfield wouldn't wonder how he got back to the house on his own, or where else he might have gone for that matter. Gregory wasn't quite ready for them to know everything.

So once he reached the house, Gregory waited outside until his breathing leveled out, and he stepped inside. Peeling off his sweaty coat, Gregory hung it up and rested against the wall for a second.

What was he going to do? Could he actually protect them from Deadlock? Or was he just putting them in more danger by staying there? Gregory fought the urge to pound his head against the wall.

Oh, for the days when Gregory just did what he was told, and he had no choices to make.

"Oh, there you are Gregory!"

Gregory jumped and spun around to face Esther. "What?" he asked, glancing around. "Oh, Mrs. Winfield." He took in a deep breath and blew it out again, scolding himself for being so jumpy.

Mrs. Winfield looked like she was about to say something when she frowned and tilted her head. "What's wrong?" she asked.

"Nothing, everything is fine," Gregory said, clearing his throat as he straightened out his shirt. "Did you need something?" he asked as he looked intently down at his snow-covered boots.

Deadlock

"Yes, I did," she said. "And if you're sure everything's fine, can you go and find Jackson?" Esther asked. "He was supposed to be back from playing by now, and I want him and Mia to help me with dinner."

Gregory glanced out the window and raised an eyebrow. "He's out there, playing in this stuff?"

"Yes," Esther laughed. "Kids do that kind of stuff."

"Right…" *Why?* Gregory wondered. The snow was cold and wet. His father made them train in it every winter, and Gregory and Grew had hated every moment of it. "I guess I'll go get him then."

Mrs. Winfield smiled. "Thank you."

Gregory nodded as he headed back toward the door and stepped outside. He hadn't gone far when he remembered he hadn't grabbed his coat, but he shrugged it off. He didn't plan on being out that long anyway.

"Jackson? What are you doing?" he called, glancing around him as he frowned. "Come on! Jackson? Mrs. Winfield wants you to come back inside!"

Why was he the one who had to track the boy down? In fact, why wasn't the boy coming back inside anyway? That's when Gregory stopped talking and a shiver ran down his spine, and it wasn't because of the cold.

Something wasn't right. "Jackie?" he called again, grimacing as he quickly swept his gaze around, and took everything in as quickly as he could. *Dear God, I don't even know if you're out there, but please protect Jackson!*

He'd barely finished the prayer when something in the snow a little ways away from him caught his attention.

They were footprints, and Gregory felt his stomach start to twist up as he moved toward them and knelt down to get a closer look at the prints.

"Men's combat boots," he mumbled, his stomach twisted up even tighter. They were the same kind he'd always worn growing up, Deadlock's standard boots, and whoever it was had Jackson.

Chapter 28

"Blast it!" Gregory spat, jumping to his feet from where he knelt beside the footprints.

He glanced back toward the house, then in the direction the prints headed. Gregory knew he didn't have time to go back to the house. If Deadlock was there, then he had to find Jackson before they did something to him.

If anything happened to the boy, Gregory knew it would be his fault, and he wasn't going to let that happen. Steeling himself, he started forward in the direction the prints went, quietly moving through the snow.

Gregory soon realized where he was going when an old barn on the Winfields' property appeared ahead of him, and he headed toward it. Once he reached the barn, he slowly pushed the barn door open just enough for him to squeeze through it.

Winter light streamed through the windows in the upper part of the barn, giving Gregory a little light as he stepped deeper into the barn and quickly scanned around him at all the dust and hay covered junk scattered through the barn.

"Jackson?" he called out, stopping in the center of the barn, with the loft looming above him. It was the perfect position for a sniper, but he didn't feel like someone was watching him from up there. Whoever was in there was on the bottom floor. "Why don't you and your 'buddy' come out, Jackie," he said, crossing his arms. "I know you're in here, whoever you are, and I'm not a barn cat, so I don't care to play cat-and-mouse in here."

A chuckling sound echoed around inside the barn. "Well, if you weren't such a hard one to track down, Gregory," someone said, "then we wouldn't have to meet like this, now would we? Trust me, I wouldn't be here if I didn't have to. I don't like the snow."

The hairs on the back of Gregory's neck stood up on end as he slowly turned toward the voice. "Wrangler," he growled, gripping his hands at his sides and really wishing that he had his gun.

"Greggy!" Jackson squealed, squirming in the man's arms. "Help me please!"

The sounds of the young boy's cries for help made Gregory feel horrible. But at the moment he couldn't show any vulnerability in front of the man; that would only make things much worse.

"What are you doing here?" Gregory asked, doing his best to ignore Jackson as he felt his face turn neutral.

Deadlock

"Hello to you too, Gregory," Wrangler scoffed as he took another step forward and pulled Jackson along with him. The boy whimpered, and Gregory wondered if he was already hurt.

Glaring at him, Gregory shrugged. "Oh, yeah. *Wonderful* to see you," he scoffed. "Now, you didn't answer me, what are you doing here? And don't give me any trash, because you know I'll know if you're lying."

Wrangler laughed. "Isn't it obvious?" he asked, grinning wickedly as he tightened his grip around Jackson. "I'm here because of you."

"Then why are you holding a hostage?" Gregory asked, taking a careful step forward and toward the two of them. "Let him go."

"And why would I do that?" Wrangler asked, grabbing Jackson by the hair and yanking his head back so he was looking toward the roof. "You know, just a little more pressure, and I could break his neck.

"Greggy," Jackson whimpered again, struggling to break free of the man's grip. But his effort just caused Wrangler to laugh.

"It's alright, Jackson," Gregory said, his eyes flickering down to the younger boy as he took another step closer. "You'll be alright. You just have to trust me."

Jackson blinked. "I do."

"Isn't that sweet!" Wrangler scoffed. "He 'trusts' you, Gregory. Does that mean he knows the truth about you?

Because I highly doubt it."

"Just let him go," Gregory growled again, gripping his fists tightly at his sides. "He doesn't know anything; he has nothing to do with this."

Wrangler shook his head. "Since you seem to care about him so much, I think he does have something to do with this," he said, sneering at Gregory. "What's the matter? Find yourself a sweet little family while you were away?"

Before Gregory could respond, he heard footsteps from the other side of the barn door. Someone was coming. *Great*! Just what he needed more civilians. What was he going to do if it was Jonathan?

He had no doubt that Wrangler would shoot him the second he saw him.

Gregory's heart thudded as he slowly turned around toward the door. *Go away!* he silently thought, hoping the person would hear him anyway. But they didn't, and a second later, a lone figure stepped through the door.

"There you are, Gregory," Cody said, pulling his hood down and shivering. "Man! It's getting cold. How are you not even wearing a coat?"

"What are you doing here?" Gregory growled, ignoring the other boy's question as he moved to block Wrangler and Jackson from his view. The last thing he needed was for someone else to get involved.

Cody ducked his head. "Look," he said. "I came here because I'd like to talk to you about what happened earlier."

Deadlock

You have got to be kidding me! Gregory thought, gritting his teeth. "Not now," he hissed out. "I don't care to talk to you."

"Why n..." His voice trailed off. "What's going on?" Cody asked, frowning as stepped to the side, and his gaze narrowed as he saw Wrangler holding Jackson anything but casually. "Gregory?"

"Nothing," Gregory said, shrugging.

Cody raised an eyebrow at him. "Well, it doesn't look like nothing."

Pinching the bridge of his nose, Gregory sighed. "Cody, just go *home*," he said. "You're not needed here." Cody opened his mouth to say something, but Gregory quickly cut him off. "Don't you have to clean *under* your *bed*, or something?"

Cody studied Gregory for a second before slowly nodding. "Yeah, alright," he said, holding his hands up in surrender. "I'm going. I'm going. Man, I just thought we could talk." Shaking his head, he slowly walked back out of the barn and vanished.

"Who was that?" Wrangler asked, loosening the arm he had wrapped around Jackson's neck.

"No one," Gregory said, turning back toward them. "And now that he's gone, he's not your problem."

"You make yourself a little friend, Gregory?" Wrangler laughed, grinning wickedly at him.

"No!" Gregory spat. "He is *not* my friend."

"Tut, tut, tut," he said, shaking his head. "Roman would be so disappointed in you. Your lying is wanting."

Gregory snorted. "Disappointed in me? Really? Is that the way you want to play this?" he asked, stepping forward. "What about Adam and Thomas? Would he be 'disappointed' in them too?"

"What about them?" Wrangler asked, squinting at him.

"They tried to kill me!" Gregory spat. "I'm sorry if I don't believe Roman didn't know something about that. I don't know what he's playing at, or how you're involved, but you're not going to use me anymore. I am *done*."

What Wrangler didn't realize was the fact that Gregory was now just a few feet away from him, and *very* mad. Carefully, he moved his left hand to his back and under his jacket where he'd kept a knife almost the whole time he'd been with the Winfields.

"Jackie," he said, looking down at the younger boy. "Duck."

The next second, he yanked the knife out and threw it toward the Deadlock operative's arm, hoping it wouldn't hit Jackson instead.

The tip of the knife cut through Wrangler's coat, causing feathers to fly into the air as it was embedded into the man's arm. He yelled out in pain at the same time as Jackson slipped out of his grasp and fell to the ground.

"Run!" Gregory ordered, motioning quickly toward the door. Jackson scrambled back to his feet and took off running. He was halfway to the door when he stumbled and fell to the ground again.

Seeming to appear out of nowhere, Cody leapt down from the loft into a pile of old hay. He scrambled to his feet, tossed something toward Gregory, and grabbed Jackson up off the ground.

Then they both headed toward the door and out of the barn.

CHAPTER 29

Gregory caught the gun Cody had tossed to him, flicked off the safety, and spun around to face Wrangler again. "You're going to let them go," he warned. "And then Deadlock's going to forget about both them and me. Understand?"

"And why should we do that?" Wrangler scoffed. "Why wouldn't I just go out there and kill the both of them?"

Without pausing, Gregory fired off a shot that just barely missed hitting the man and tore through the edge of his coat. "Because I won't miss next time," he said, giving him a small smile. "And I think your self-preservation is higher than that."

Wrangler opened his mouth to respond, but before he could, there was a 'pop!' of another gunshot, and the man crumbled to the ground.

Gregory wasn't quite sure what the sour feeling in the pit of his stomach was when he realized the man was dead, but he didn't like it. But knowing he wasn't the one to shoot the man caused Gregory to tense and quickly scan around him.

"Now, that was not the way I trained you, Gregory," came a voice from across the barn. "You should at least have shot him in the leg."

"Roman," Gregory whispered, staring at the man as he stepped forward from the other side of the barn and out of the shadows. He hadn't expected him to be there too, and Gregory felt fear sweep through him.

"You've gotten yourself into a sticky situation, haven't you? But your father, he doesn't need to know about any of this, Gregory," Roman said, motioning around them. "I'll take care of everything, and you don't have to worry about a thing."

"I'm sorry, Roman," Gregory whispered, lowering his gun as he held his head up high. "But I... I can't go back there. Besides, why do you even care? You tried to kill me!"

Roman sighed and shook his head. "It was only part of your test, fool!" he spat. "But it wasn't supposed to send you off your rocker like this!"

"I'm not off my rocker," Gregory said, shaking his head. "I just want out, and... and I think Grew should leave too."

"If you want to throw your life away, fine," Roman growled. "But Grew stays. Deadlock will need a leader when your father dies. It should be you, but if not you, then it will be Grew. I will make sure of it."

If his brother stayed, that wasn't his fault. But even with

that reasoning, Gregory still felt guilty. "Come on, Roman," he said, rubbing his head with his free hand. "We're just kids, and you want us to be adults."

"I used to think you were the smart twin, but I'm starting to think I was wrong," Roman said, shaking his head. "You have never been 'just kids', and you will learn that, one way or another. At least now I know where both yours and Grew's loyalties *really* lie."

Gregory frowned at him. "What are you talking about?"

Laughing, Roman shrugged his shoulders. "Who do you think informed me of what was going on here? How you seem to think this *little* family can give you a 'home'," he scoffed. "I never would have thought you would be so easily fooled."

"Grew…" Gregory whispered. "He… he told on me?"

"You're acting like he told your father you took the last cookie," Roman said, shaking his head. "You betrayed us; of course he told me so I could help you." He laughed. "It would seem I chose the wrong twin to train. Grew knows where his loyalty should lie."

Gregory laughed. "Are you kidding me right now? What 'loyalties' do any of you truly have?" he asked, narrowing his eyes at his former mentor as he tightened his grip on the gun even as he held it at his side. "Tell me, Roman, did you know about my mother?"

For a second, Roman's gaze faltered. "This has nothing to do with your mother," he growled. "This is about you and

Deadlock

your brother."

He knew the man was trying to change the subject, but he gave in anyway. "This has *nothing* to do with Grew."

"Oh, but it does," Roman said, smirking. "You're lucky, he had every right to kill you instead, but he didn't. Because I think a small part of him hoped you'd come back. You have no idea how much he cares for you, Gregory. He would have done almost anything for you."

Gregory blinked, then slowly shook his head and ran his hand through his hair. "Obviously not anything," he whispered, his gaze flickering to the ground. "I'm sorry, Roman, but... I can't go back. I don't belong there, and I doubt Father's even noticed I'm missing. I know it won't be easy, but just let me go!"

Roman let out a long sigh as he rubbed his chin. "If that's what you really want," he said. "Then you can walk away *after* you finish your testing."

"I... I can't," Gregory stammered, taking a step back. Anymore, the thought of killing Jonathan turned his stomach. "I can't take my target out. I won't."

Anger flickered across the older man's face as he gritted his teeth and took a step toward Gregory. "You will," he growled. "You will take the target out, and I will make sure of it. I didn't train you *all* your life for this."

Shaking his head, Gregory took another step back. "No!" he said. "And you can't make me. I'm not your little pawn, Roman, and you can't just make me do whatever you want. *I am done!"*

"Are you disobeying an order, Gregory?" Roman asked, tilting his head as he raised an eyebrow.

Gregory's heart started to thud. It was one thing to just leave Deadlock and not finish his mission; it was another thing completely to disobey a direct order. He couldn't ever come back from this.

Squaring his shoulders, his dark eyes locked with Roman's. "Yes," he whispered, standing a little bit taller. "Yes, I'm disobeying an order. I am *done.*"

Roman looked at him in surprise, then he gave Gregory a patronizing smile. "I don't think you fully understand what you're doing, boy."

It was in that moment something seemed to change in Gregory, and he truly looked at the man he'd called a mentor for as long as he could remember and saw him for what he really was.

"And I don't think you actually know *me*," Gregory growled, taking a step closer to Roman this time. "You think I'm just a kid you can push around? But I'm not a kid; you made sure of that. You touch any of the Winfields, and I'll make you regret it."

To Gregory's surprise and frustration, Roman looked at him and laughed. "Are you threatening me?"

"Yes, I'm threatening you," Gregory said, smiling as he began to play with the gun in his hand. "And it's quite sad I have to explain that to you. Aren't you supposed to be the smart one?"

"Very well," Roman said with a sharp nod. "If that's what you want, who am I to stop you?" With that, he pivoted around and marched back toward where Gregory imagined there was another way out of the barn.

He didn't go too far before he stopped and glanced back toward him. "You would have been a great leader, Gregory," Roman said, shaking his head. "But obviously you're too weak for that position."

Gregory gritted his teeth but didn't rise to the bait. "Goodbye, Roman. I hope I never see you again."

"Don't worry, you won't," Roman chuckled, glancing to the side at something Gregory couldn't see. "Take care of him."

As soon as the words left his former mentor's mouth, Gregory knew exactly what they meant, and he reacted accordingly. Time seemed to slow down as Gregory's training instinctively kicked in.

The next second, the air was torn by bullets flying toward where Gregory had been just a second before. But by then, he'd rolled across the dirt-covered ground and behind an old tractor parked against the side of the barn.

There was the sound of metal hitting metal as bullets smashed into the tractor.

Gregory pressed himself against the cold metal body of the tractor, squeezing his eyes shut as he calculated where the shots were coming from. From what he could tell there were five of them, three up above in the loft and two below.

They must have entered some time while he was talking with Roman because he knew there was no way Cody would still be alive right now if they'd been up there in the loft with him.

Finally, there was a pause in the shooting

"Five-to-one," he mumbled, his eyes still closed. "Could be worse." With that thought in mind, Gregory shoved himself up and pivoted around, and fired the shot aimed up at the loft above him.

He heard a yell, and one of the operatives dropped, clutching his side as he tumbled over the edge and fell to the ground, but by then Gregory was ducking behind his cover again as the shooting started once more.

Chapter 30

For Gregory, the next several minutes turned into a blur of dodging, firing, and recalculating his aim. Finally, he'd worked it down to two-to-one, but the last two seemed to be more cautious than the other three.

Popping the magazine out, Gregory grimaced when he realized he only had a couple of bullets left. He'd have to use them sparingly and hope that the other two operatives didn't have any extra clips.

Leaping out from behind the tractor, Gregory rolled across the ground and behind a pile of junk. The three seconds he was in the open allowed him to spot his target hunkered down behind what Gregory guessed was a spare shovel for the tractor.

He couldn't just stay there; he had to do something. This was his fight, and he needed to end it. Gregory knew he was still outnumbered, but it was looking much better that he might survive this than it had just a couple of minutes before.

Taking in a deep breath, he looked around him and mapped out a plan of attack. Though he still didn't know where the other operative was, and that fact alone unnerved him. He hated unknown variables.

But whether Gregory knew where he was or not didn't change the fact that he needed to take the other operative out. And the best way he could think to do that would be a straight forward assault.

Without letting himself procrastinate any longer, Gregory tightened his grip on his gun. Then, grabbing onto the top of the junk he was hiding behind, he propelled himself over the top of it, careful not to cut himself on any of the rusty metal.

Once on the other side, he hit the ground, rolled, and came up on his knees just as the operative looked up over the edge of the shovel. In a split second, Gregory aimed and fired, hitting the operative in the shoulder and sending him reeling back.

Before Gregory could even lower his gun, the last Deadlock operative appeared on top of the tractor above him. The next second, the operative leapt down toward Gregory, throwing them both to the ground, and sending Gregory's gun skidding across the ground and under the tractor as they started to fight.

Gregory kicked out at the man as he scrambled back and tried to climb to his feet, but the man was faster than he expected and was soon on top of him. Kicking and punching, Gregory tried to fight him off.

But because Gregory wasn't even thirteen yet, the man's size quickly won out, and he soon had Gregory pinned to the ground. It became obvious that the man had run out of bullets as he drew a knife from his belt.

"Traitor!" the man spat. "I'm going to kill you, then I'm going to kill that lästige family, very slowly. Enjoying every second of it."

Gregory opened his mouth to say something, but before he could, the man let out a low grunt before falling on top of him. Gregory let out a small 'yelp' before shoving the man off of him and looking up at the person standing above him, holding a crowbar in his shaking hands.

"Cody," Gregory whispered, staring at the other boy. That's when his adrenaline decided to drop back to normal, making him slightly nauseas. "Ich hasse mein Leben," he grumbled, pinching the bridge of his nose as he pushed the dizziness back.

When he opened his eyes again, Cody was still standing above him. "Thanks," Gregory whispered, grimacing.

"Yeah, you're welcome." Cody glanced around, his gaze moving from one moaning and bleeding operative to the next. "Are… are you okay?" he asked, frowning as he let go of the crowbar and it clattered to the ground.

"I'm fine!" Gregory said, waving the other boy off as he scrambled to his feet and quickly glanced around. "Where's

Jackson?"

"Oh, right," Cody said, snapping his fingers. "He's hiding in one of the snow piles. Outside."

Gregory nodded, then he moved to grab his gun from under the tractor and passed Cody as he headed out to find the younger boy. He barely even felt the cold wind blow against his jacket as he stepped outside, and goosebumps appeared on his arms. "Jackie!" he called, looking around him. "You can come out. It's just me."

"Oh, Greggy!" Jackson cried, scrambling over a snow pile and throwing himself at Gregory. The next second, Gregory had an armful of a crying boy.

"I'm sorry," Gregory whispered, bending down and burying his face into the eight-year old's thick, dark hair. "I never meant for any of this to happen. I'm so… so… sorry." The next second, unease hit him.

"Watch out!" Cody yelled out at the same time. But the warning came a second too late. Gregory tried to turn and protect Jackson with his own body. And in one fluid movement, Gregory drew the gun out from behind him, swept it around, and fired at the man.

But two shots went off at the same time.

Gregory felt it cut through his side, then Jackson yelled out in pain as the Deadlock operative crumbled to the ground and Cody bolted to grab his gun. But Gregory barely noticed as he tossed his gun away and lowered Jackson to the ground.

Deadlock

Hardly even thinking about what he was doing, Gregory quickly pulled off his jacket as the dark stain on the boy's coat began to grow. *Oh my gosh, he's been shot because of me, he's going to…*

Gregory didn't let himself take that train of thought any further as he worked to stop the bleeding with his jacket. From what Gregory could tell, the bullet had missed any vital organs, but if he didn't get help quickly, he would still die.

"Jackie, just hang in there," Gregory said, speaking softly as he applied pressure to the wound and Jackson cried out in pain. "I'm sorry."

"It hurts," Jackson whispered, grabbing onto Gregory's shirt with his hand.

"I know," Gregory whispered. "But I have to put pressure on it." He found his eyes burning and he didn't know why. "You're going to be okay, you hear me? You've just got to hang in there for me."

"He needs a doctor," Cody whispered to Gregory from where he was kneeling beside him, causing Gregory to flinch. "You know that, right?"

It was then Gregory realized how out of it he was; he hadn't even realized that Cody was sitting there until he'd started talking to him. He'd never missed something that obvious before.

"I've already called for help, but I'm calling 9-1-1 too. Okay?" Cody asked, and when Gregory nodded, he jumped to his feet and bolted toward the house.

Gregory had no idea what '9-1-1' was, and at the moment, he didn't care. He had other things on his mind as he turned his full attention back to the younger boy, knowing he might not be awake for much longer.

"Hey, Jackie, you're doing great," he whispered, smiling down at the younger boy as he carefully moved him closer to keep him warm. "You're way braver than most people. You know that, right? When I was your age…" *I was learning how to shoot people like this.* "I wasn't nearly this brave."

"Re…ally?" Jackson mumbled, his eyes flickering closed for a second. "But, I'm… I'm… not brave."

"You are to me," Gregory said, swallowing as the boy's eyes slid closed again. This time, Jackson didn't open them again. "Jackie?!" he said, shaking him lightly, but the younger boy didn't respond, and Gregory knew why.

He wasn't very big, which meant blood loss would happen faster. He was going into hypovolemic shock, and there was nothing Gregory could do.

"Oh, God," Gregory prayed, squeezing his eyes shut as he felt the sticky warm feeling of Jackson's blood soaking through his jacket. "If You're punishing them because of me, please don't." He opened his eyes and looked up at the sky as he held Jackson a little tighter. "Don't let Jackson die because the Winfields are good people, and I'm… not. If You're going to punish someone, punish me. Let me die, not him. He's just a kid!"

Deadlock

Gregory's mind barely registered the sound of sirens not far away or the sound of someone driving up behind him. He didn't actually realize the ambulance was there until the EMTs came running up to him.

"We'll take it from here, son," one of the older EMTs said as he knelt in front of Gregory and Jackson and they were all set to work on him.

Gregory nodded as he let them take Jackson from him, and he quickly moved out of their way. It was at that moment two of the cops and one of the EMTs pulled the operative who had shot Jackson to his feet.

A flare of anger hit Gregory at that moment, and if the police hadn't been there, he wasn't sure what he would have done to the man. As it was, it took a lot of self-control for him not to pick up his gun again.

Instead, he took in a deep breath and moved toward one of the officers as the EMTs carefully put him onto a stretcher.

"There's…" Gregory swallowed as the officer turned toward him, and memories of being told to avoid cops at all cost hit him. He quickly pushed it down and forced himself to look the officer full in the face. "There are four more men inside the barn…"

His attention was drawn back to the ambulance as Jackson was lifted inside, and Gregory spotted Mr. and Mrs. Winfield running toward it. Though one of the EMTs held up a hand and stopped them. "Please, only one person," she said. "But we need to hurry."

"Go," Mr. Winfield said, kissing his wife's cheek. "I'll be there as soon as I can."

Without any hesitation, Mrs. Winfield nodded and climbed into the back of the ambulance. The door was slammed shut, and they took off, sirens blaring.

CHAPTER 31

Gregory looked down at the blood-covered ground and squeezed his eyes shut. He knew once the Deadlock operatives were in custody, it would only be a matter of time before the police started asking him questions, and he had no idea how he was going to answer them.

"Are you hurt?" The question from Mr. Winfield broke Gregory out of his thoughts, and he glanced over at the man.

"No, Mr. Winfield, I'm fine," Gregory lied, ignoring the burning in his side as he turned his gaze away from the man. "I… I wasn't the one who was hurt."

"Are you sure?" Mr. Winfield asked, placing his hand on Gregory's shoulder. "Holy smokes, kid! You're freezing!"

Yanking himself away from the man, Gregory actually started to realize how cold he was. Maybe it was the adrenaline or something else, but he hadn't paid much attention to it until now.

Rubbing his hands over his arms, he shrugged. "I forgot

my coat in the house," he said. "And Jackson… he needed my jacket more than I did." He glanced toward where the jacket had been tossed away, and he tasted bile in his mouth.

"Oh," Mr. Winfield said, turning slightly pale as he cleared his throat. "Then let's go inside, huh? I… I don't want you freezing to death out here." He glanced toward the police officers. "Is it alright if we go inside? You can come in and ask your questions when you're done out here."

One of the officers nodded. "That would be fine." Mr. Winfield nodded his thanks, and they both headed inside. It wasn't until they reached the house that Gregory wondered where Cody had gone off to.

"Daddy!" Mia cried, flinging herself at Mr. Winfield the second he stepped through the door. "What's going on? Why's Jackson going in that strange car?"

"Because he was hurt, honey," Jonathan said, sweeping her up into his arm as he kissed her cheek. "But… but he's going to be okay." Gregory grimaced, but the little girl obviously didn't hear the hesitation in the man's voice.

They didn't know that Jackson was going to be alright.

"Who… Who hurt him?" Mia asked, her dark eyes growing large.

"I did," Gregory said, not even thinking about what he was saying. Mr. Winfield looked over at him and blinked.

"Mia, honey," Mr. Winfield said, sitting her down again. "Why don't you give me and Gregory a moment to talk,

Deadlock

okay?" Mia hesitated before nodding and dashing up the stairs to her bedroom. "Did you shoot?" Mr. Winfield asked, turning toward Gregory. "Did you shoot Jackson?"

"No," Gregory said. "I might as well have because it's my fault those men were here in the first place."

Mr. Winfield sighed. "So those men... they're Deadlock?" Gregory nodded. "And you're the one who took them out? How?"

"Because that's what I've been trained to do my whole life," Gregory whispered, looking away from Mr. Winfield. "I don't know what you might think, but Deadlock doesn't mess around." He spun around to face Jonathan again. "I... I didn't come here to keep an eye on you, Mr. Winfield. I was sent to kill you."

To Gregory's surprise, Mr. Winfield just nodded. "Then why didn't you?" he asked, studying Gregory.

"Oh, I don't know," Gregory scoffed. "Maybe because I'm weak and cowardly, and I couldn't do it."

Mr. Winfield took a step toward him. "From what I've seen, you're not weak or the least bit cowardly."

"What do you know?" Gregory snapped, glaring up at Jonathan. "You don't know anything about the world I come from. You..." He squeezed his eyes shut. "This... this is why I can't stay. We're from two different worlds, and I'll never be able to have a normal life."

"Gregory..." Jonathan started.

"Don't! Just... don't. I don't want to hear it," Gregory

said, shaking his head. "Once we know what's going to happen to Jackie…son, then I'll be out of your hair forever. For now, I'm… I'm going to go wash up," he said, realizing his hands were still covered in Jackson's blood and it turned his stomach.

Without waiting for Mr. Winfield to respond, Gregory sprinted to the bathroom and slammed the door closed behind him.

His hands started to shake as he turned the water on and began to wash the blood off, scrubbing hard at his hands. It was an appropriate metaphor; Jackson's blood was on his hands.

If the little boy died, it would be Gregory's fault for staying with the Winfields when he knew he shouldn't.

Gripping the edge of the bathroom counter, Gregory gulped in the potpourri-filled air, fighting the urge to smash the mirror with his fist. Who was he fooling? He knew he couldn't stay with the Winfields, so why did he let himself even entertain the idea?

And now a little kid was in the hospital, possibly dying, because of him. Gregory groaned and squeezed his eyes shut. A moment later, a knock on the bathroom door pulled Gregory out of his reverie.

"Gregory? You in there, dude?" Cody asked from the other side of the door.

Without a thought about what he was doing, Gregory yanked the door open and glared at the other boy "Did you need something?" he growled. "Because if you don't, just leave me alone."

Gregory moved to close the door again, but Cody was blocking it with his foot, and he didn't look like he was about to move it. "We can either have this conversation out in the hallway or right here," Cody said. "I don't care which it is, but we are going to talk."

Crossing his arms, and hiding the grimace the movement caused, Gregory glared at him. "And what conversation would that be?"

"Well, for one thing, that's not all Jackson's blood, is it?" Cody asked, his gaze flickering down to Gregory's torn and bloodstained shirt. "If you're not going to tell Mr. Winfield about being hurt, at least let me take a look."

"I don't know what you're talking about," Gregory whispered, his hand involuntarily moving to his side as he dropped his gaze to the ground, too tired to do this anymore.

Rolling his eyes, Cody shoved the door open and stepped toward him. He pushed Gregory's hand away as he pulled the side of the shirt up. He grimaced when he saw the flesh wound the bullet had caused, before hitting Jackson.

"Yeah... practically a paper cut," Cody huffed as he let the shirt drop back down. He moved over to the cabinet under the sink and opened it, searching around inside it until he pulled out a package of bandaids and a bottle of hydrogen peroxide.

"Don't use the hydrogen peroxide," Gregory grumbled as he leaned back against the wall. "I… have some cayenne pepper in my boot." He grimaced as he realized how much his side was hurting him.

Cody stopped and frowned at him. "Okay…" He knelt down and pulled a small packet out of the pocket on the side of Gregory's combat boots. "Why am I using cayenne pepper instead of hydrogen peroxide?" he asked as he stood up and tore the packet open.

"It will stop the bleeding," Gregory said, rubbing his hand across his face. "Disinfect it, and help it heal faster. "

"Of course you would know that," Cody grumbled, shaking his head as he bent down. "Hold your shirt up for me." Gregory reluctantly did as he was told as he readied himself for what he knew was coming.

He started counting and controlling his breathing as Cody applied the cayenne pepper to the wound. The burning in his side instantly intensified, and he fought the urge to punch something. "Trottel!" Gregory spat, glaring at Cody. "I think I felt better when I was just leaving it alone."

Cody rolled his eyes. "Don't be such a big baby," he said as he pressed one of the bandaids over the wound, careful to make sure the skin was closed first.

"You've done this before," Gregory commented, studying the other boy.

Deadlock

"I've been banged up myself a time or two," Cody said, shrugging as he stepped back and Gregory dropped his shirt. "Wish I knew cayenne pepper was supposed to be better than hydrogen peroxide; it's what I always used to use. Sorry you got hurt."

Gregory sighed and shoved himself away from the wall. "It doesn't really matter; I deserved it."

The next second, Gregory ducked Cody's swat to the back of his head. Without thinking about what he was doing, he grabbed Cody's wrist and twisted it around behind Cody's back.

"What do you think you're doing?" Gregory asked, before letting go of Cody and crossing his arms.

Rubbing his shoulder, Cody turned back toward him but didn't seem all that surprised by Gregory's actions. "Well, I was hoping to knock some sense into you," he growled, glaring at Gregory. "You're such an idiot. You just turned on Deadlock for this family!"

Gregory turned pale. "How do you know that?"

"I heard your conversation in the barn," Cody admitted, ducking his head. "You weren't exactly being quiet about it." He cleared his throat and looked up at Gregory again. "Now that your wound is taken care of… um… there are a couple of people here to talk to you downstairs. But you might want to change your shirt first."

CHAPTER 32

After changing into a new shirt, Gregory found himself in the living room, staring down at his hands as he tried to ignore the looks Jonathan and the two FBI agents were sending his way.

Somehow White and Huntley must have gotten the police to leave the investigation to them, though how they'd gotten there so quickly was slightly unsettling. After leaving him to change, Cody had disappeared again, leaving Gregory alone to explain what had happened.

When he knew he couldn't put it off any longer, Gregory started his story from when Mrs. Winfield sent him to get Jackson, skimming over parts of his conversation with both Wrangler and Roman.

There was a short pause once he was finished before anyone spoke, and Gregory prayed once more to the Winfields' God that He wouldn't take Jackson from them.

"Where'd the gun you used come from?" Agent White asked, breaking the silence from where he sat on the other couches beside Agent Huntley.

"It was mine. I sent Cody to get it," Gregory whispered, knowing there was no reason to deny it. "But you won't find any identifying marks or numbers of any of the guns. We manufacture our own weapons, including guns and ammunition."

Agent Huntley nodded. "We had some suspicions about that."

"Why do you have a gun?" Mr. Winfield asked, resting his elbows on his knees as he bent forward.

Glancing around, Gregory took one of the throw pillows and wrapped his arms around it, even though he knew he was giving away how nervous he was about all of this. "Where's Mia?" he finally asked.

"I decided to put her down for a nap before we leave for the hospital in a couple of hours," Mr. Winfield said. "So are you going to answer my question?"

Taking in a deep breath, Gregory nodded. "It was... the one I was given to..." He cleared his throat, and he hated it when he felt his cheeks start to burn. "You know, to do the job I was sent here for."

"Oh..." was all Jonathan seemed able to say.

"Was there anything else you wanted to know?" Gregory asked, looking around at the three men. "Come on! It's not a very good interrogation if you don't interrogate me."

Agent Huntley shook his head. "This isn't an interrogation, Gregory," he said. "We just want to know what happened."

Gregory snorted. "Please! I know that you know who I am," he said. "I'm just surprised you've let me go this long without throwing me into prison."

"Look," Agent White said. "You're right, we know who you are, and what you're probably capable of, but from what Cody tells us, you're also a good kid. We all know that we can't choose what families we're born into."

"Wait," Gregory said, narrowing his eyes at the agent as he held up a hand. "Did you just say, 'from what Cody tells us'?"

Agent Huntley sighed and leaned back against the couch. "I figured you'd catch that," he said, shaking his head. "Alright. You can stop lurking outside now!" Huntley called out. "Come in here and join the conversation."

Somewhat hesitantly, Cody stepped around the corner and entered the living room. He shoved his hands into his pockets and glanced toward Gregory, grimacing before he turned toward Agent Huntley.

"Sir," Cody said, with a nod to Huntley even as his eyes flickered over to Gregory again.

Agent Huntley gave him a small smile. "It's alright, you have permission to tell him the truth."

"Thank you, sir," Cody whispered, dropping his gaze as he turned toward Gregory. "Look, Gregory," he said, rubbing the back of his neck. "What happened earlier... I um... things are complicated for me. I've done some things

Deadlock

I'm not proud of."

Gregory had a feeling that he already knew where this conversation would end, but he didn't want to admit it, even to himself.

"You mean like whatever you were smoking earlier today?" Gregory asked, crossing his arms even though he was slightly glad the conversation had shifted away from him, at least for the time being.

A small smile tugged at Cody's lips. "Sugar."

Gregory blinked. "What?"

"That's what I was smoking," Cody said. "Sugar. Agent Huntley gave me a second chance I didn't think I'd ever get, and… I help them with things they can't do themselves."

"You mean you're a CI?" Gregory said, shoving himself to his feet. "You work for the FBI." He snorted and threw his hands up. "Wow! I can't believe it. You double bluffed me, and I fell for it! You really were sent there to see if I was a psychopathic killer."

"Yeah, okay?" Cody said. "What do you want from me? Do you want me to confess? Like I've done something wrong? Because I haven't!"

"No, I was the idiot who thought you actually wanted to be my friend," Gregory spat, shoving Cody back a step. "Well, turns out you're just like the friends my father warned me about. Backstabbing users."

"Oh, right," Cody scoffed, stepping back toward Gregory. "Because I'm sure your father has a lot of experience with 'friends' between terrorist attacks and murders. I'm sure he's a great person to go for advice."

How could he say that? He didn't know anything about his father, and he sure as heck had no right to say anything about him.

With a yell, Gregory kicked out at him, and he slammed his still booted foot against Cody's leg. The other boy yelped in pain as his knee buckled, but even as he stumbled back a step, Cody punched Gregory in the stomach.

Gregory cursed in German. "You're going to pay for that," he growled, taking a step toward Cody.

"Stop it, Gregory. You're not the only one in the world who knows how to fight, you know," Cody growled. "But if I really wanted to hurt you, I'd go for your side."

"Oh, please!" Gregory scoffed. "You got in one lucky shot."

"Boys, enough!" Mr. Winfield snapped, jumping to his feet. "I won't have fighting like this inside my house," he said, stepping between them. "Do I make myself clear?" he asked, glancing between the two of them.

Both boys reluctantly nodded and stepped back from each other.

"Ich hätte nie gedacht, dass ich dir vertrauen könnte," Gregory growled out, glaring Cody down. He'd been stupid to even think he could have gone to this other boy about Deadlock coming for him. If he had, he might as well have told the FBI himself.

Deadlock

"You know what?" Cody said, matching his glare. "I don't think I want to know what you just said to me."

Gregory snorted and crossed his arms. "Well, in that case, I said, I never should have thought I could trust you!"

Cody flinched. "That's not fair."

"Why not?" Gregory asked. "Because you've been playing me the whole time we've known each other?"

"Gregory," Agent Huntley said, standing and placing a hand on both boys' shoulders. "Cody was just doing his job."

"Oh, do shut up, Uncle Justin," Gregory spat, shooting a glare toward the FBI agent as he yanked his shoulder free from his grip. "I don't remember inviting you into this conversation."

Cody blinked. "Wait, 'Uncle'?"

"Oh! So your little handler doesn't tell you everything, does he?" Gregory said, fake pouting. "Then let me enlighten you. Agent Huntley, unfortunately, is in fact, my uncle."

"It's true, Sheldon," Agent Huntley said, looking much older than he had earlier. "Gregory is my sister's son."

"'Sheldon'?" Gregory repeated, glancing between the two of them. "Oh! So you lied to me about your name too. I guess I should have figured."

"No! Sheldon is my last name," Cody said, stepping toward Gregory. "I try to get him to call me 'Cody', like everyone else, but he never does."

"Well, you should get used to it if you hope to become an agent when you're older," Agent Huntley said, shaking his head at his CI. "You won't be going by 'Cody' then."

"You want to work for the FBI?" Gregory said, snorting. "Well, you should do great; you're obviously good at fooling people."

Cody dropped his gaze. "I'm sorry," he whispered. "I… I didn't know you considered me a friend. But I honestly didn't mean to… betray you, if that's what you think. They just wanted me to keep an eye on you and see if you were… dangerous. I really am sorry. Will you forgive me for having to lie to you?"

For once, Gregory actually wasn't sure how to respond. No one had ever apologized to him before.

CHAPTER 33

Cody was actually asking him for forgiveness? Gregory looked at the other boy and the honesty in his eyes, and that's when he broke. Letting out a small whimper, Gregory dropped to the ground, pulled his knees to his chest, and buried his face between them.

Pull yourself together! Gregory yelled at himself as he felt his body tremble, but he just couldn't. Why were all these people being nice to him? They had every reason to hate him, but they didn't, and he didn't understand it.

"Um... what did I do?" Cody asked above him.

"I don't think it was you," Agent Huntley said, sighing. "He's just a kid who's obviously been through a lot. Why don't we... you know." No one said anything, but Gregory heard the sound of three sets of footsteps leaving the room.

Someone was still there.

"Gregory?" Jonathan said, and Gregory felt a hand on his shoulder. "Hey, buddy, do you... do you want to talk about it?"

Gregory shook his head, even though his chest ached as he pulled his arms tighter around his knees. "I can't go back," he whispered as he squeezed his eyes shut. "And I can't stay here either."

"Whoah!" Mr. Winfield said, squeezing his shoulder as he knelt next to him. "Who says you can't stay here?"

"You... you will," he hiccuped. "If Jackson dies, it's... it's my fault! None of you are safe with me here."

"Gregory," Jonathan said softly as he ran his hand through Gregory's hair. "You were sent here to kill me, I understand that, but I think God had other plans for you. I also think that if your father had sent someone else, I would probably be dead right now."

Gregory didn't want to admit it, but it was probably true "They're... they're not going to just let me walk away," he said as he slowly looked up at Jonathan. "I can't stay here; I'm a liability."

"No, you're not a liability," Mr. Winfield said, shaking his head. "You're a kid who's had a really messed up childhood. And... I know I speak for everyone when I say, we still want you to be a part of this family."

Staring at the man, Gregory tried to decipher if the man was telling the truth or not. "Even after everything that's happened?" he finally whispered, grimacing as he ducked his head again.

"Families don't give up on each other that easily, I'm afraid," Mr. Winfield said, then he cleared his throat.

Deadlock

"Gregory, can I... can I give you a hug?" he asked. "I understand if you don't want me to."

Somewhat reluctantly, Gregory looked up at him again and blinked. "A what?" he asked, tilting his head as he frowned at Jonathan.

Mr. Winfield grimaced, then without warning (or maybe his question had been one?), he wrapped his arms around Gregory and pulled him against his chest. Gregory let out a small 'yelp' not sure what to do.

"You're just a kid, Gregory," Mr. Winfield whispered, kissing Gregory on the top of his head as he continued to hold him. "You don't have to do everything on your own, and not everything that happens is your fault."

Gregory hated crying in front of other people, but he couldn't seem to stop himself as he buried his face deeper against Mr. Winfield's chest. Whether it was a vain attempt to hide, or something else, Gregory didn't know.

If his father were there, he would have been in so much trouble for making himself so vulnerable in front of others. "You're... you're nothing like my father," Gregory mumbled, slowly pulling away from him.

Mr. Winfield chuckled. "No offense," he said, giving Gregory a small smile. "But from what I've gathered of the man, I think I'm going to take that as a compliment." Gregory didn't say anything, and Jonathan scrambled to his feet, holding out his hand to him. "Come on."

"Where... where are we going?" Gregory asked,

ignoring the man's hand as he reluctantly stood.

"I'm going to go grab Mia, then we're heading to the hospital," Mr. Winfield said. "Hopefully they'll know what's going on by then." Gregory nodded as he followed him out into the hallway, where Huntley, White, and Cody were waiting.

They all turned toward them as soon as they stepped through the doorway. "We um… good?" Huntley asked, looking Gregory over. "I'm not good with the whole 'emotional' stuff."

Mr. Winfield chuckled and ruffled up Gregory's hair. "Well, I think that might be genetic," he said with a wink before turning toward the agents again. "Um… It's not that I don't trust you guys, but I'd rather you weren't in my house while I'm gone."

"Alright, we're out of here, Jonathan," Agent White said, shaking Jonathan's hand. "Let us know if there's anything we can do for you." With that, he turned and headed toward the front door.

"Um…" Agent Huntley cleared his throat. "The same goes for you, Gregory. If you need anything… Well, you've already got my number." With that, the three of them were gone, and Mr. Winfield headed upstairs.

Gregory hesitated a second before hurrying out the door after them. "Cody," Gregory called out just before the other boy was about to climb into the car. "I… I forgive you."

Deadlock

The other boy stared at him for a second before grinning and giving him a nod. Then he climbed into the car, and they drove away.

Going back inside, Gregory grabbed his coat, and by then Mr. Winfield had Mia ready to go. They got into the car and drove in silence to the hospital (partly to do with the fact that Mia was half asleep).

Once at the hospital, it didn't take them long before they found Mrs. Winfield and another woman Mr. Winfield said was from church. Gregory did his best to go unnoticed as Jonathan hurried up to his wife, carrying a sleeping Mia.

Slowly edging his way forward, Gregory sat down on one of the chairs against the wall and watched as Mr. and Mrs. Winfield began to talk.

"The doctor said Jackson was very lucky and that the bullet missed any vital organs," Mrs. Winfield said, her eyes red from crying. "They… they say he's going to be alright, and in a few months as good as new. In fact, he's already woken up, though he was a bit groggy."

Gregory had already known that the bullet hadn't hit any vital organs. What took the doctors so long to figure it out? It was frustrating, but at least Jackson was going to be okay. There wasn't much more he could ask for right now.

He was in his own thoughts and didn't notice when the lady from the church took Mia and left for the night. Nor did he notice Mrs. Winfield moving toward him after

Mr. Winfield had spoken to her for a couple of minutes.

Though he did glance up from where he was staring intently at the ground when her shadow fell over the tiles he was looking at. "Mrs. Winfield," he said. "I… I assume Mr. Winfield told you what happened?"

She nodded and took the seat next to him. "Yes, he did," she said. "Though, I imagine he probably left some parts out." Esther sighed and placed a hand on the top of Gregory's head, gently turning him to look at her. "I know you haven't known us for very long, but since the moment you walked into our lives, God has been laying it on our hearts to adopt you. You've made yourself a part of our family, whether you meant to or not. We love you, Gregory."

For a long second, Gregory just stared at her. "I…" He grimaced and ducked his head. "No one's said they loved me since my mom died."

Mrs. Winfield kissed him on the forehead. "Well, it's true," she said. "Jonathan explained to me what happened, and none of us blame you for Jackson getting hurt. In fact, from what the doctors and EMTs are saying, we have you to thank that he's still alive. Most thirteen-year-old boys wouldn't have known what to do in a situation like that."

"Most 'thirteen-year-old boys' wouldn't have put your family into a situation like that in the first place," Gregory said. "Those… those men were there for me. It's my fault he got shot."

"Oh, honey," Mrs. Winfield said, pulling him closer to

her, and Gregory fought the urge to pull away. "None of this is your fault, and the doctors say Jackson's going to be okay. God was looking out for both of you today."

Gregory ducked his head. "Right."

"Come on, there's someone who wants to see you," Mrs. Winfield said, taking Gregory's hand and pulling him to his feet.

Before he could put up a protest, or even asked her where she was taking him, they were standing in front of one of the hospital rooms. Mr. Winfield sat beside a bed holding a pale, small looking Jackson.

Jonathan rose to his feet, kissed Jackson on the forehead, and nodded to Gregory, before both he and his wife stepped out into the hallway, leaving the two boys alone in the hospital room.

For a long moment, Gregory just stood there, awkwardly staring at the ground.

"Greggy?" Jackson mumbled. "What's wrong?"

Those three words broke Gregory out of the fog that seemed to have surrounded him, and he looked the little boy in the face. He couldn't remember ever being as innocent as this boy was.

"Hey, Jackie" Gregory whispered, stepping forward and kneeling next to the bed. "Look, I'm... I'm sorry. It's my fault you're in here. Those... those men with the guns were there because of me. I... I understand if you hate me."

"Are you kidding?" Jackson mumbled, giving Gregory a

weak smile. "This is awesome! None of the other kids at church are going to believe I survived a gunshot wound."

Gregory gave him a wet laugh. "That's… that's good," he said, giving the younger boy a small smile. "I'm still sorry it happened." He moved to stand up, but Jackson caught his hand with his.

"You're not leaving, are you?"

Even though he didn't think the boy meant permanently, Gregory hesitated to answer, then glancing toward the door where Mr. and Mrs. Winfield both stood watching them, Gregory shook his head. "I'm not going anywhere, Jackie."

It was then that Gregory realized, thanks to his testing, he'd found something he'd never expected.

A home.

See more of adult Gregory Winfield in: Phantom Thief (AKA Simon Lee book 1).

How far would you go?

Even at a training base in the middle of nowhere, you can't escape the war raging across the solar system.

He wasn't looking to become a superhuman.

Your power doesn't define whether you're a hero or a villain, but it's the choices you make that define you.

Also, by **P.D. ATKERSON**

<u>AKA Simon Lee</u>
Phantom Thief (book 1)
Christmas Hostage (book 1.5)
Guardian Eagle (book 2)
Murphy Lawson (book 3)
Ghost Hunter (book 4)
Most Wanted (book 4.5)
Winnie Winfield (book 5)
Not Enough (book 5.5)
Rebel Mind (book 6)

COMING JULY 1ST 2021: Nicholas Bishop (book 0.5)

<u>Of the Stars</u>
Testing (book 1)
COMING NOVEMBER 27th 2021: Wandering (book 2)

<u>An Accidental Superhero Story</u>
The Villain's Hero

P.D. Atkerson is a homeschooled writer, living in Montana. She spends almost as much time in the worlds she creates as she does the real one.

When she's not reporting the stories of Simon Lee and other heroes, she's making ice cream, learning Russian or traveling to different worlds through the portals of books. She has a black belt in sarcasm and a master's degree in useless facts.

For behind the scene info check out her blog at https://pdatkerson.blogspot.com And for fans of AKA Simon Lee tap the 'Top Secret' on the top right on the page for special content.